A GATHERING OF THE MOROSE

A Gathering of the Morose

by

Simon Kurt Unsworth

Black Shuck Books
www.BlackShuckBooks.co.uk

Versions of the following stories first appeared as follows:
'Coel Coeth' in *Strange Gateways* (PS Publishing, 2022)

Cover design & internal layout © WHITEspace 2025
www.white-space.uk

First published in the UK by Black Shuck Books, 2025

978-1-917173-97-1

A few months before I put this collection together, my cousin Gabriel Birchill died at the far too young age of 23. I never knew the adult Gabe but I knew the baby and child Gabe and he was a happy, fun little guy. I wish the world could have seen more of him, and he more of the world. This book is dedicated to him, and to those he left behind – Pip and Martin, his mum and dad, Nic, Oliver and Lucy, his brothers and sister, Meryl and Harry, his aunt and uncle, Pete, James and Edward his cousins and Barry, his granddad. I know Gabriel lives in their hearts and memories even if he isn't there for them to hug any more.

Ave atque vale, Gabe. I wish I'd known you better.

Here be dragons...

And then the streets were full of monsters.

Holding Allie's hand, Harding walked the lanes and pavements of the place of her birth and watched as children of all ages went from house to house and demanded treats. He saw spiders with bouncing hairy legs, and creepy clowns holding balloons, and aliens. He saw several children with the bobbing insectile antennae on springs, the sort that he'd called 'deeley boppers' when he was young, on their heads, a brace of witches, a veritable army of zombies and one small girl made to look like a drowned woman. She had limp, wet hair, painted blackness around her mouth and eyes and her skin blanched down to a fishbelly pale, a costume that seemed to Harding somehow both elegant and sad and yet terribly adult and inappropriate. They carried baskets and bags of sweets, these monsters, giggling and chewing as they walked, adults shepherding the younger beasts, leading gaggles of them in crocodiles across the roads and along pavements.

Older children ran unsupervised, their disguises more perfunctory, masks over heads but no attempt at costumes except for the teen uniform of hoodies and jeans. Mostly they ignored everyone but their own age group, although one teenage boy did run up to Harding and Allie wearing a mask fashioned into the face of an old man, and rubber finger extensions with ragged, long nails that he waved at their faces while cackling evilly. Given that the rubber fingers were filthy, and that the worst threat the boy could make was to offer to prepare a meal whilst wearing them, Harding was going to shoo him away empty handed, but seeing the look of enjoyment on Allie's face he dug out a handful of chocolates from his pocket and handed them over. How Allie looked at him when he did it was reward enough, a treat he hoped to sample later.

They strolled through Halloween, Harding and Allie, and enjoyed each other and the world around them.

Later, as the streets started to empty, Harding assumed they'd be going back to Allie's parents' house, where they were staying for long weekend. He hoped to be able to pull Allie into a pub or restaurant on the way back, to spend time with her somewhere warm and snug, huddled into a corner head next to her head so that he could smell her closeness and tell her he loved her, but instead she pulled him to the village's outskirts and started up into the hills.

"Where are we going?" he asked as she walked ahead of him, her hand holding his as though needing to pull him. He didn't really mind the change of plans or where they were going, to be honest; just being with her was enough. A hillside somewhere unpronounceable in Wales was as good as anywhere else, and better than most because they were alone except for each other. In the evening's moonlit darkness the curve of her buttocks in tight denim and the sweep of her thighs were magnificent to behold, and when she turned back the light caught in her smile and made it something beyond beautiful, something endless and alive, turning her eyes into glimmering silver pools that he felt he could let himself fall into and willingly drown in.

Towards the top of the hill Allie pulled Harding off the path and towards a copse of old trees whose trunks were gnarled and twisted, the weight of their crowning leaves and branches pulling them down into crone shapes. In amongst the trees the air was warmer, smelling of moss and clean, damp earth and something else, something sharper that reminded Harding of winter nights from his childhood. It was the smell of bonfires, and it increased as they pushed further into the darkness. They slowed, Allie still ahead, feeling with their feet for roots and other obstructions, stepping over and around until at last they came to a clearing in which a fire burned.

It filled most of the space before them, a circle of heavy stones in whose centre a mass of wood had been reduced to glowing orange embers. The heat of it was heavy and damp, making Harding sweat and forcing him to open his coat, the smell of it thick with sap and leaf and ash. Apart from the fire, the clearing was empty.

Well, almost empty. There was a cairn of small stones to one side of the fire. Allie let go of Harding's hand and went to it, picking up two stones and handing him one. From a pocket in her jacket she took a sharpie and wrote something on the stone, then turned and threw it into the fire. When she turned back to him she was smiling, but the smile looked old, somehow, and tinged with something he couldn't identify. Melancholy? Sadness? Something vaster than her and him, anyway. A recognition of their smallness against the walls of the universe. She was holding the pen out to him and he took it saying, "What am I supposed to do with this?"

"Write a prayer on the stone and throw it into the fire."

"Allie, I'm not religious, you know that."

"It doesn't matter. This is *coel coeth*, and it's a tradition we have. It's a Welsh thing, I think. Some places do it on Bonfire night and I think some do it on the winter solstice, but here we've always done it on Halloween," and she dropped her head so that her chin was against her neck and her eyes were peering out at him from suddenly shadowed brows and intoned hollowly, "when the barriers between this world and the others are at their thinnest."

She lifted her head and her eyes were bright again and she was smiling. "Now, city boy, you write your heart's desire on the stone, a prayer or a wish or whatever, and you throw it into the fire and God, or the universe or our own will or the fairy folk or whoever it is that controls these things, decides if it's a good wish, if you're worthy enough, and if you are the whatever makes it come true."

"Really?"

"Really."

"Who lights the fire?" he asked, intrigued, thinking about what to write. What did he want, really? What did he want his life to be? What didn't he already have? What did he need?

"No one knows," Allie replied, still smiling, but now it was broader, happier, the smile of someone enjoying herself. Suddenly, Harding thought he might be being taken for a ride and lowered stone and pen.

"Allie, how can you not know? Someone must come up here to get the fire pit ready, bring the wood and light it, and they must do it early so that it's down to embers for this time of night. Someone must put the stones in a pile for people to use."

"Maybe they do, but I don't know who it is and no one ever talks about it. And not everyone comes up here, only people who want something, and there's never anyone else here when you come up and you never see anyone on the way to or from the clearing. It's how it's always been. Now, write your prayer or wish."

Harding though for another moment then wrote across the stone's rough surface, throwing it into the fire by Allie's stone when he had finished. "Now what?" he asked.

"We wait a few minutes," Allie replied. "Be thankful you didn't have to do this a few years ago. When I was a kid we had to write on the stones with the burned end of a stick in ash, so your prayers or wishes or whatever had to be really short. We'd just have to write things like 'Money' or 'Love'! Once, I came up and wrote 'Sex' on a stone, can you believe it? Just that, just 'Sex', and it took ten minutes to get it legible. Sharpies have made things easier, and a damn sight more eloquent."

"Did it ever work?"

"Well, I have sex with you, don't I?" she asked, and he could hear the tease and salacious grin in her voice even though he couldn't see her face because she was leaning towards the fire, a mere silhouette against the wavering orange heat.

"What are you doing?"

"Getting the stones," she said, and he saw she was using a stick to roll the stones to the edge of the pit and then up over the surround. When they fell to the ground, two glowing eggs of fire, she used the stick to push them into the earth where they made the damp mud steam gently and crackle as it dried. "While we're waiting for them to cool, was there something you wanted to ask me?"

"Oh," he said, and then, "do you want to go for a drink on the way back?" through a suddenly dry mouth.

"The other question," she said, and stepped close so that she was pressed against him, head tilted back and looking up at him, the heat of her greater than the heat of the fire. Her lips parted slightly as she looked at him and her tongue traced across the edge of her upper teeth. "Well?"

Harding leaned down so that his mouth was just over hers and, very quietly and on an exhalation so that his breath passed into her, said, "Will you marry me?"

"Yes," she replied and they kissed then and for a glorious moment they were the only things in the universe, in all of time and space there was just them and the kiss and the future they had just decided to share, and when they broke the kiss the moment stayed in the air around them and settled into Harding's skin like smoke, like the tattoo of a promise.

Later, after he and Allie had had not just a drink but a meal to celebrate, and had told her parents, who made them have another drink, they went up to the room they shared and started to undress. They were down to their underwear when Allie said, "Wait, there's another thing we have to do!"

"What?"

"Come with me," she said, digging something from her coat pocket and pulling him from the room into the hallway. Uncomfortably aware of his near-nudity he tried to resist but she was inexorable, leading him into the bathroom. She turned on one of the taps so that water flowed into the sink and then held up the two stones, now cool and ashy and muddy. Gesturing at him to hold his hand out, she dropped one into his upturned palm and said, "That's yours."

"How do you know?"

"Just do. Now, you have to wash it." So saying, she held her stone under running water, rinsing it clean, and then held it up before him again, showing him that its surface was unmarked. No trace of the writing remained. "The universe has agreed, or God has answered my prayer, or granted my wish. Whatever, I'm good. Now you."

Harding washed his stone and found it also unblemished. "Looks like I lucked out too," he said and grinned at her. "Now, shall I take you to bed?"

"Yes, please," she said, "and make it good, but keep it quiet. I don't want my parents to hear."

"Of course," he said, and took her back to the bedroom, and they were quiet and it was as good as it had ever been between them and just at the moment he lost himself inside her he thought, *She's my fiancée, we'll be together forever and this is how life will be* and it was the finest thought he'd ever had.

The next morning they lay in, relaxing. He woke before her and watched her for a time, enjoying the steady rise of her chest and the way her face slackening in rest, the faint lines of concentration that usually creased her forehead smoothed away to nothing. She was beautiful, he'd always known that, but now her beauty seemed enhanced by the love he felt for and from her, turning her into something that seemed almost inhuman in its glory. *I hope all people in love feel like this*, he thought, smiling inside at his soppiness even whilst he enjoyed it.

Allie mumbled something and moved slightly, and that was when the spider scurried up onto her face, across her cheek and stopped, nestling into the curve made between the top of her nose and the arc of her eyebrows.

It seemed huge, its abdomen hairy and bulbous, its legs arched across her cheeks, its feet on her forehead and lower face, and its eyes glittered with reflections that looked as deep and endless as stars circling distant galaxies. It had fangs, curved scythes jutting from a black maw below those eyes, and it seemed to be looking at him, recognising him, knowing him. Harding, too stunned to make a sound, jerked back and the jerk woke Allie up. Her eyes opened, peering at the spider's underside. She swore distractedly and raised a hand up, and before he could stop her she knocked the creature away. It fell back, disappearing behind her as she rolled to face him.

"Jesus!" he finally managed to gasp and pulled her towards him.

"Frisky," she said, "but let me wake up first. It's too early, you haven't even brought me a cup of tea in bed yet."

"There was a spider, it crawled up on your face," he said, looking warily behind her and trying to see the bastard thing. "It was huge, looked like a fucking tarantula."

"Was that what it was? Oh well. We're in Wales, you get used to nature not respecting your boundaries, but a tarantula? I don't think so. It was probably just a wolf spider, they get pretty big and this time of year they come inside looking for a mate, trying to get in a last desperate shag before the winter kills them. We're used to them out here in the country, but they obviously still scare you soft city dwellers. Tarantula indeed! Now, where's my tea?"

Was that it, he wondered as he made them drinks, padding around her parents' warm kitchen, *was I scared by a big house spider? I mean, do they grow that large? Was it that large, or did I just blow it up into something it wasn't because I'm not used to them?*

They had tea in bed and then made love again, enjoying the lack of responsibility, and then went downstairs for breakfast where Allie told her parents about the incident. Eventually, because Allie didn't seem bothered and her parents laughed with her when she told them and all three took to calling the creature 'Harding's Tarantula', he joined in the laughter and accepted that he simply wasn't used to country living. Still, when they were back in the room dressing he made sure that he jerked the duvet on the bed back and banged around the room loudly to scare the spider away. 'Harding's Tarantula' it might be, joke it might be, but he didn't want to see it again.

He hadn't bought a ring because he hadn't planned his proposal, so they went shopping that morning and Harding spent a frightening portion of his monthly salary on a delicate diamond engagement ring, and then they went for a drink. They found a pub that was quiet and shadowed and ordered food, and then Allie left Harding to go to the lavatory. Sitting in a comfortable seat in a booth, he started to think forward. Marriage. He tasted the word, liking the feel of it in his mouth, liking the texture and depth of it. He wondered about their future, about what it would contain. They didn't live together yet, had never even discussed co-habitation or children, all that was to come, and he found himself looking forward to it all, no matter what it ended up looking like. He was just beginning to grasp the enormity, the *rightness*, of what they had chosen to do when the shadows at the base of the bar moved.

The pub wasn't full but there were people in it, other diners, and their legs and the chairs and tables blocked the movement after he first saw it, crowding it out in shuffles and strips, but then it came again. Something was slipping along the floor in the space below the foot rail that ran along the bar. The something was long and low, gliding along serenely among the feet and legs, apparently undisturbed by the people around it.

Was it a dog? A rat? *Jesus*, Harding thought, *is that a rat?*

No. It moved too smoothly, like a fast-flowing spill of water. It was long, too long to be a rat, stretching two or three feet although he still couldn't make it out. It was as though some darker patch had displaced the usual shadows, was cutting through them below the brass rail, moving along silently, heading deeper into the pub with some purpose only it knew.

Coming closer.

At the corner of the bar, instead of following it around, the shape turned and started out across the open floor towards him. No one else seemed to react, the people at the tables between him and it or the people at the bar ordering, collecting drinks, none of them saw it and they should, they *should*, because it was a thing that shouldn't have been, *couldn't* have been, because now Harding could see it clearly.

It looked like a trilobite, broad and squat, its segmented black carapace gleaming dully, hundreds of legs just visible around its edge scuttling it across the expanse of scuffed wooden boards. Antennae on the front of what Harding had to assume was its head dipped and swayed as it came, feeling out its route. Harding wanted to move but found he couldn't; the sheer oddness of seeing the thing had locked him in place. Was it a joke? A dog or cat in a costume, some expensive Halloween toy like the drones that he saw people fly sometimes? An elaborate trick?

The thing stopped. Its front end reared up, flexing back, segment of its armoured hide disappearing under segment as it rose, revealing on its underside a downturn sickle mouth full of tiny, bitter teeth. Like the spider, it seemed to be looking directly at Harding and still no one else reacted to it, no one else saw it and oh Christ what was it, what was it this thing scuttling impossibly across the floor? Harding wanted to scream, wanted to run but movement seemed lost to him, as though the strings between his brain and muscles had been cut. It hissed then, mouth opening wider and a sound emerging like air escaping from a punctured throat, shrill and wet.

It dropped and moved again, arrowing at him. When it reached the table closest to Harding it vanished under it, losing itself among the feet of the diners seated there. Its absence broke whatever spell had been holding him and Harding shuddered, letting out a ragged breath. He snapped his feet up off the floor, hearing a tiny wail emerge from his mouth, all the noise he could make, and watched the point where he expected the thing to emerge.

Nothing.

After a moment, Harding ran a shaking hand over his face. Adrenaline flooded his system and he began to shake, his wail turning into a series of broken hitches, aware that the people nearest to him were looking at him curiously, and then Allie's hand was on his shoulder and she was sitting beside him and saying, "What? What's wrong? Sweetie?"

When he'd caught his breath, snatching it out of the air in long gasps, Harding managed to calm himself and speak. "Is there something under the table?"

"Our table?" asked Allie, looking down.

"No, that one," said Harding, pointing, ignoring the people sitting at the table who were now staring openly at him.

Allie bent, peering under the table, before sitting up. "There's nothing there except feet and legs and dust," she said quietly. "Babe, what's wrong?"

"I saw…" he said before trailing off. What? What had he seen? An insect the size of a child moving like an oilslick across the floor. "I don't know."

"You don't know?"

"No. I mean, I saw something but I don't know if it was there, or if I saw it right. I can't have done, I don't think."

"You mean you hallucinated it?" asked Allie and ran her hand along his arm. "Has it happened before?"

"No. I mean—" and there was a thump as the waitress set their food dishes down, ending the conversation.

Food, even though Harding wasn't hungry any more, seemed to ground him, anchoring him back into this reality where Allie was his wife-to-be and the worst thing on the bar floor was mud from the hillwalkers' boots. By the time they'd finished, the insect seemed like a memory of a thing half-seen through screens of glass and muslin, something unreal. Allie looked at him all the time they were eating, and when they finished said, "If you're having second thoughts you can just say. I don't want you to do anything you don't want, and I don't want the thought of marrying me to make you hallucinate." She was smiling as she spoke but her voice and eyes were serious.

"What? No," he said. "God, Allie, marrying you will be the best thing I'll ever do. I just had a moment. Not about you," he added hastily, seeing the look on her face.

"A moment?"

"Let's go outside and walk," he said, "and I'll tell you." And he did, everything from the spider again and how large it had seemed to the insect scurrying at him across the floor. When he had finished, Allie was silent for a minute before she spoke.

"And it's not some elaborate ploy to disentangle yourself from me?"

"No. God, no."

"Well, we've both been working hard," she said, and it was true, they had. They'd met a few months ago whilst working in a coffee shop and both were working other jobs, Harding as a office cleaner and Allie in a restaurant in the evenings. "Maybe the stress of it's got a bit much? Plus, you're a city boy at heart, maybe the country air has affected your brain?"

"Maybe," he said, and realised he was smiling because that what Allie could do for him, make him smile no matter what.

"Don't go insane, sweetie," Allie said. "Not yet, anyway. Let's have a few sane years, shall we?"

"If you insist," said Harding, still smiling, and as they walked he tried not to think about spiders and insects the shape of teardrops with mouths like downturned screams.

In the middle of the night, Harding woke because his legs and arms ached. It was a shooting, wavering pain that seemed to pulse out from his elbows and knees to fill his skin like hot water.

He rolled out of bed, careful not to wake Allie or make a noise that might disturb her parents. Walking eased the pain a little and he stepped quietly around the room, going to the end of the bed and back again and waving and bending his arms slowly. His joints popped as he moved, the noise reminding him of his father and grandfather, of the noises of their aging. He wondered if he was getting old, felt the dull ache still festering in his muscles, and thought that he probably was.

Finally Harding stopped by the window. Carefully, so as not to let any light fall on Allie and disturb her, he parted the curtains and peered out at the street beyond. Allie's parents lived at the foot of one of the hills – not the one that the fire they had cast their wishes into had been on, but still a significant lump of landscape. It blocked the night beyond it, a black mass between Harding and the rest of the world, its flank furred with trees and foliage just visible in the glow of the lights from the street. *I could get used to this*, Harding thought, *no cars or distant sirens, no half-eaten kebabs left on the doorstep or pissed clubbers puking and screaming. Maybe we should end up somewhere like this, where there's peace and space and we can breathe.* Harding pressed his forehead against the glass, liking its coolness, letting his gaze soften, looking not outside but in, thinking nothing but future thoughts.

There were people in the trees at the bottom of the slope.

They were just beyond the treeline, perhaps forty or fifty yards past the wire fence that separated the hill from the street, and Harding knew immediately that they weren't walkers or late night revellers, they belonged to the place that the insect and the spider belonged to. Because yes, the spider belonged there too, he knew that now. Something in his world had fallen off-kilter, and the figures were the latest manifestation of it, of his mental illness or whatever it was. Three of them, hunched and cowled, they moved through the trees, seeming to dance and jig yet never revealing themselves except for the flash of something pale, a skinny wrist or gnarled hand, as they threw their arms up and their robes fell back.

Robes? Yes, robes, black robes that hung to their feet, robes with hoods that rose to jagged points behind their heads and formed ovals of darkness where their faces should be, robes that flailed and flapped, witches' robes. They were witches, the figures, witches taken from some child's fairy tale, clichéd and nonsensical but real enough because he could see that they were kicking grass up, flicking it from their feet and out towards the road. Harding started to laugh at the absurdity of it, at the terror of it, of these three witches – who were undoubtedly crones as well under those robes – dancing along the outskirts of a Welsh suburb, laugh as though his chest might split and his teeth clack together and break.

"What's wrong?" asked Allie from behind him and Harding laughed harder, trying to stay silent, tears leaking from the corners of his eyes, and gestured her to him. He heard her rise and the sound of her footfalls, gentle against the carpet, and then she was pressing against him.

"I'm going insane," he said through the laughter and tears. "I'm sorry, I tried to wait a few years but clearly I failed. I'm going mad."

"Really?" asked Allie, and then said, "I'm not so sure, sweetie, because if you think you're mad because you can see three prancing jokers in the trees then I must be going mad too."

It took a second for what Allie had said to sink in, and then Harding said, "You can see them?"

"Three of them," replied Allie, "dancing. They aren't coming out into the light but I know they're there."

"Yes! Yes!" said Harding. "Dancing! And there was an insect before!"

"Well, let's not go too far," said Allie, moving away from him. He continued to watch the figures as a series of rustlings and shufflings came from behind him. Out in the trees, the figures capered.

"Here," said Allie, coming back to Harding's side and handing him his jeans and a jumper. "Let's go and see what's going on."

The woods were dark. *Isn't that the start of a poem, or story, Harding thought? Isn't it the start of most fairy tales, the woods are dark and the path through them long and hazardous, and once upon a time there was a lost child or a betrayed adult?* Which role was he here, stumbling amongst the trees following Allie, following the noises, her hand in his as ever? Child or adult?

Something flashed ahead of him, pale and sickly in the darkness, crablike. A hand? An upturned face, cowl falling back as the dance grew more frenzied?

Again, more of the pale flashes now, hands and faces, yes, all of them, the three figures solidifying out of the gloom, their dance a jumbled and capering thing visible in the light from the stars and the moon, the gleam outlining the shadows of robes as knees kicked up high and arms rose and fell, as heads rolled back to face the sky and then dropped again and as they came closer Harding realised that there was chanting, or singing, some low and sonorous sound that gave the night a voice.

"Hey," called Allie, lifting the small torch she'd brought with her and sending the beam at the three figures.

"He arrives," called back a hoarse, cackling voice and the three figures stopped and the glade they were in was suddenly full of light, more light than the torch could create, blazing light that etched them with hard edges and birthed long, reaching shadows. Each of the three turned to face Harding and Allie and then raised an arm, pointing at them. The one in the centre threw their head back, flicking the hood away, to reveal a pallid face framed by straggling hair, the eyes sunken and the nose hooked and bony. It was a woman, and when she opened her mouth her teeth were weathered, blackened tombstone stumps. She wailed, and the other two joined in, pointing directly at Harding now, and the sound was full of threat.

"Who the fuck are you?" asked Allie, stepping forward, ignoring the brightness of the light.

"We are us," said the woman, somehow wailing the words, elongating each one so that it stretched and yawed from her mouth, "and we come for him."

The fingers were extended now, clawed and filthy nails itching the air between them and Harding.

"Me?" he said. "Me? What have I done?"

"You called," the woman said again and then the light blinked out, and in the dizzying flash of afterimage, the figures turned and darted away, disappearing into the trees and flowing from sight. On the ground, impaled with pins, lay a doll that looked vaguely like Harding, the only evidence they had ever been there.

Later Harding and Allie sat in her parents' kitchen drinking coffee, the doll on Harding's knee. Allie had pulled the pins from it and Harding's aches had immediately dissipated. They looked at each other for a long time before Allie said it.

"They looked like witches to you?"

"Yes," said Harding, thankful that she'd brought it up, that she'd seen it too.

"How do you know?"

"How do I know what?"

"That they were witches?"

Harding opened his mouth to answer and then closed it again. How *had* he known? He thought about it, and then said, framing it halfway between a question and a statement, "Because they looked like witches?"

"How, though? How did they look like witches?"

"Because they looked like witches are supposed to look. They had ragged robes, and bare feet, and their hair was messy. The one whose face we saw was ugly and had a hooked nose."

"And warts."

"And warts," he agreed.

"But that's odd, isn't it? Because witches aren't like that, not in real life, are they? At least, I can't imagine they are. I mean, have you ever met anyone who looked like that? Those three, they were like the clichés of witches, what witches are supposed to look like," Allie said, "based on all the fairy tales and Disney films and whatever. It's like they were playing at being witches. And the doll is like a cliché of what witches do."

"Yeah," said Harding because Allie was right, they'd looked like how you'd describe witches if you were asked about them, acted how they'd act if you made up a witch for a story. "So they were joking? Being stupid?"

"No," said Allie. "No, I don't think they were, and that's what doesn't make sense. People dressed as clichéd witches, and threatening you. Do you think it was actually you they wanted? They can't, can they? I mean, they presumably picked you at random because you were the first person to come along?"

Harding, looking at the doll looking back at him from his knee, said nothing.

~

Then the dead came.

It was their last full day with Allie's parents and they had a meal planned for that night – Harding was cooking something spicy, he had told them, but had not yet decided what – and they were walking to the local shop to browse ingredients for him to make a final decision. The shop was small and inspiration sadly lacking, so Harding had come to the conclusion that a basic curry might be best when he happened to glance at the front of the store and out through the windows to the street beyond.

There was a zombie shuffling along the other side of the glass.

It was a man, old, his hair dragging in wisps over a near bald, greying scalp. His mouth was open, pulled down at the corners as though the man had had a catastrophic stroke that had somehow plucked the muscles from his lips, which drooped, revealing yellowing, dry teeth. Harding watched, wondering if it was someone late for Halloween, or a prank was being played on someone, as the man, the zombie, lurched forward, one leg dragging. He swung a shoulder sideways, bumped against the shop window and slid along it, leaving a smear that looked as dry as mothdust. When it, when *he*, reached the shop doorway, the man turned and looked in the store, his eyes glazed and pale. His head jerked as he stared, twitching like some palsied marionette, until his gaze fell on Harding.

The dead man smiled. It was a terrible thing, a rictus straining at the edges not to become a grotesquery, lips peeling back and splitting as the smile stretched across the dead man's face. Dust, or something like it, spilled from his mouth, and then he moved again.

He sloped into the shop, arms rising, one shoulder lower than the other, tongue lolling from its twisting mouth. It never took its gaze off Harding as it shuffled along the first aisle, bumping into other shoppers who didn't seem to notice, moving around the zombie, stepping out of its way and then carrying on browsing and taking items from the shelves. Harding, still unsure of what was happening, tapped Allie on the shoulder, drawing her attention from the various sauces that they had moments before been trying to choose between.

"Can you see that?" Harding asked her, nodding at the man who had now reached the end of the their aisle and was starting to shuffle determinedly along it. He bumped into a display of cans and they fell, rolling across the floor. A shop assistant came and started picking them up, ignoring the shambling thing just ahead of him.

"Yes," said Allie, her voice small.

"Good," said Harding, "it's not just me then. Is it real?"

"Yes," said Allie, not hesitating. "It's a dead man. A zombie."

"Jesus. What do we do?"

Allie took Harding's hand and led him to the far end of the aisle, past shelves of wine and beer, the zombie still plodding after them, and went into the next aisle. This one led back down to the shop's door and they walked fast along it, still holding hands, still hearing the sounds the zombie made, the low moans and the drag of its feet as it shuffled along. They reached the door and pushed past people to get through it, going out into the street and the sunlight beyond. Harding went along the front of the shop so that he could see up the aisle they had been in.

The zombie had gone.

Shoppers picked items, the assistant was still restacking the spilled cans, the basket they had abandoned was still on the floor at the end of the aisle, but the dead man was gone.

"What's happening?" asked Harding. "Am I going mad? Are you?"

There was another groan, like thunder collapsing against distant hills, and when they turned another zombie – a woman this time, and fresher, blood still dribbling from a wound in her scalp and spilling from the dragging intestine dripping from the tear in her belly – was staggering along the street towards them. As they watched her feet became tangled in her own guts and she fell, hitting the ground hard. After a second, her head came up and she stared at Harding, then moaned again and started to pull herself along the ground towards him.

"Come on," said Allie and pulled Harding, leading him away from the crawling woman back towards her parents' home. As they went, walking quickly but never quite breaking into a run, she said, "You aren't mad, because if you were I wouldn't have seen it, but I did, just like the witches last night, and I did see them and I did see the two zombies just now. There's something odd going on, man of mine."

"Odd," echoed Harding, marvelling at how inadequate a word that was to describe these last few days.

"Odd," repeated Allie firmly, "but we'll work out what it is, this odd thing, and we'll sort it. After all, I've only just got my wish and got you to ask me to marry you and I'm not having anything mess it up now. Not zombies that apparently only we can see, or bugs, not *anything*."

Harding stopped. Allie pulled on his hand again but this time he didn't move, still except for his lips which were pacing out words, framing an idea that seemed absurd yet oddly right. "Allie," he said, "what did you wish for on Halloween night?"

"What?"

"What did you wish for? Up at the fire? In that coelacanth thing?"

"Coel Coeth," Allie said, giggling, and he loved her then more than he ever had, felt a wash of emotion so powerful it was almost breathtaking because she could still laugh, despite the dead and the women in the trees and the insect that she hadn't seen but that she believed he had seen, could still laugh, and he knew he needed her by his side forever because if she could laugh, he could laugh, and if they could laugh then everything would be okay. "I wished for you. For you and me to be together until the very end."

"Just that?"

"What more do I need?"

Harding thought, still chewing an idea, trying to mulch it down to something manageable, something understandable. Allie had wished for him and he'd proposed that night, something he'd been planning to do anyway but hadn't it suddenly felt right, suddenly felt more than right after she had thrown the pebble into the fire? Yes, yes it had suddenly been right, the rightest thing ever.

And what had he written?

"Allie," he said, "I think I know what's happening. I think. It's the coel coeth thing, what I wrote and what the fire granted."

"But that's just a silly tradition, it's not real."

"Isn't it? Your wish came true, didn't it? I wrote a wish and I think it's been granted."

"Well, what did you wish for?"

"We'd had such a lovely day, been together, and it had been so much fun, and I'd not left your side all day and I didn't want that to stop."

"Babe, what did you write?"

"I asked for the day not to stop. Allie, I asked for Halloween with you to never end."

The climb felt harder this time, the way steeper and the ground more uneven.

They had gone back to Allie's parents' home first, the journey thankfully uneventful. No more of the dead appeared, although Harding thought he saw shadows massing in an alleyway and once Allie had jumped at something she had seen but he had not, dismissing his querying look with a wave of her hand and a smile that looked distinctly shaky. At the house, they had gone to the bedroom and drawn the curtains so that the street outside and anything it contained could not see them, made coffees and sat and talked.

It made no sense.

It made exact sense, because all the things Harding had seen on Halloween night he had seen since, hadn't he, but made into an odd reality. The spider on Allie's face, the insect in the pub and then the dead, that staple of modern Halloween, all pasty faced and deep-eyed and mangled. Had there been something else he had seen? He couldn't remember despite Allie's questions. "Forewarned is forearmed," she told him, "if we're going to get through this with no more surprises.

"How do we get through it," Harding asked, "how do we stop it?"

Harding's first plan was to get in the car and drive, back to the city and to lights and noise and kebabs spilled on the street and clubs that let out their punters at five in the morning like vomiting whales, but Allie argued against it. "It's bad enough here," she said, "but imagine if it comes with us. Imagine trying to track zombies though rush hour or bugs on the northern line on a Saturday night."

The next plan was to ignore it. This was Allie's idea, because as she said, nothing had actually harmed either of them. "Not yet," Harding had said, remembering the way the insect had hissed at him and the way both of the dead had reached out for him. They hadn't hurt them because, what, they hadn't reached him? Because this thing, whatever it was, was building up, creating a reality in which it came closer and closer before finally closing with him and taking hold? And what then? Eaten by an insect, or a zombie, Allie dead through the venomous bite of some ghastly spider? No. Ignoring it was not an option Harding liked.

"Can we fight it?" asked Harding.

"What, kill the zombies or insects? Well, if no one else can see them you'd look like you were attacking the air, you'd be locked up and then you'd be easier for it to get. Or you'd be attacking a normal person who just looks like a zombie, and you'd be arrested. No, that's not the way. I wonder if we're looking at this wrong?"

"In what way?"

"Well, maybe the solution is in the origin. I mean, why? Why you?"

"I don't know," said Harding truthfully. He wasn't, he didn't think, a bad man. He tried to live a good life, he didn't hurt people, he tried to treat people they way he wanted to be treated. Shit, he even gave to charity. "I'm a decent man, I think."

"You are, you're my good man," said Allie, taking his hand. "So. Pissed off any old Welsh gods recently? Missed an appointment with any wicker men?"

"Not to my knowledge," he replied, grinning despite everything, "unless you can piss off the old ones by doing something innocent?"

"Oh, I'll bet you can piss off the old ones in any number of ways," said Allie. "You can probably do it just by breathing in an odd pitch on the wrong day of the week, or walking in the wrong direction over an old grave or something. Well, if you can't think of anything, we'll have to ask the fire, won't we?"

"The fire?"

"The fire. It started this nonsense, it can help us end it."

It was a long journey, moving along tiny streets, heads down, avoiding the rambling, staggering dead. The streets were filling with them now, all of them seeming to move their heads in lazy swivels, trying, Harding assumed, to catch sight of him. Thankfully, they seemed as dense and lifeless as the zombies in the bad movies he and Allie sometimes watched, and as slow moving, and none had chance to do more than glance at them before they were passed and gone. At one point a knotted mass of the dead blocked the street ahead of them, but Allie knew an alleyway that connected to a narrow passage along the side of two houses and they avoided them without too much difficulty.

There was another insect at the end of the passage, and this time Allie saw it. The two of them froze as it scuttled by, not looking in their direction, its body low and segmented, long antennae bobbing before it as though tasting the pavement. It hissed as it went, a long, stretched sound like the run-out groove noise of the singles of Harding's teenage years. "They're not looking very hard for you," whispered Allie, "are they?"

"No," said Harding, feeling oddly guilty, as though it was his fault.

"It's like the purpose is in the appearance, not in the catching of you, it doesn't make sense. Let's go," said Allie after another moment when nothing had appeared in the exit from the passage. They went, scurrying in the opposite direction to the insect, reaching the wooded slope without further incident.

And the hill was steep.

The path to the clearing that the fire had been in was covered, the tree branches forming an interlocked ceiling above Harding and Allie, the trunks to either side of them seeming to grow thicker and denser the further they went. Harding could feel the effort in his calves and thighs, and the air was full of the sound of things crackling and treading around them. He saw shadows moving in the peripheries of his vision, saw the dead closing in and spiders dropping from above them, grotesque bodies dangling from silken thread, fangs pregnant and dripping with venom, saw ripples in the earth's covering of rotting leaves shifting and moving as buried insects flowed through the dankness like mouthed torpedoes, yet when he looked around they were gone, the leaves dripping with nothing more than old rain, the earth humped with nothing more threatening than twisted roots and stems. Harding tried to keep his eyes down, looking at nothing but his feet, but still the world was clustered with threatening shadows as all the Halloween monsters crept closer and closer until he thought he would burst, thought he would scream, and maybe this was the point, maybe the point was to drive him mad rather than have him eaten by corpses or torn apart by impossible creatures, and then he was screaming, aching and screaming inside his closed mouth and Allie was holding his hand and saying, "It's okay, honey, it's okay. We're here."

The glade was dark, the fire almost burned to nothing now, but there was still heat here, heat and the dull orange glimmer of embers in the centre of the pit. "If it's Halloween every day, the fire has to burn," said Allie simply when Harding wondered, aloud, how the fire was still alive. "It's what you asked for and got, isn't it?"

"I suppose," said Harding. None of this made sense and he was simply rolling with it now, rolling in the centre of the fever dream day. Allie handed him a pebble and a sharpie and said, "Write a new wish."

"What should I write?"

Allie didn't reply, simply looked at him with what they had both taken to calling *the stare*, the look that said, *Don't be an idiot.* "Oh, yeah," he said, smiling despite everything, and scribbled over the pebble. Using a stick, he knocked a hole into the heart of the remaining fire and pushed the pebble in, covering it even as its surface was blackening and heating. They waited, holding hands, Harding looking helplessly around him at the trees and the shadows and hearing the approaching noises again even as Allie said, "There's nothing there."

"No?"

"No. Trust me."

"I do."

"Good. It's time." Allie went to the fire and dug into it, using the same stick Harding had, dragging the stone to the edge of the pit and up the small wall much as she had the other night, then forcing it into the mud. A tiny curl of steam rose from it along with a sweet, earthy smell. They waited another minute then Allie dug the stone from the earth, handing it to Harding who put it into his pocket. He kept his hand around it for a second, trying to feel through its covering of ash and mud whether the words were still on its surface even as he knew it was pointless; all he felt was grit and the slimy residue of burning.

The way back was worse. Whilst they had been up on the hillside, the streets had filled and now the bugs moving among the dead. Here and there were small grey aliens, eyes large, although Harding didn't remember seeing children dressed up as aliens on Halloween night. Perhaps they had been there and he'd seen them without seeing them, he thought, the same as he must have seen children dressed as clowns, because there were clowns on the streets as well, painted grins wide on faces that looked to have melted and bubbled and dripped down to create elongated masks that didn't quite hide the tombstone teeth that filled their mouths. Allie and Harding went along back streets, ducking behind walls when they needed to, once crouching behind a car as a cluster of the dead moved along the centre of the road, and all the while people on the pavements and in cars saw nothing, moved out of the way or slowed down without apparently realising it, and Halloween bloomed again.

Allie's parents were out, thankfully, so they went straight to the bathroom. In the harsh light, Harding's face looked pale in the mirror and Allie's looked worse, wan and curdled like old milk. He took the stone from his pocket and ran it under the tap, washing away the mud and ash. He thought about doing this the other night, the two of them in their underwear and happy, thought about the night they'd had and the time they'd had since, and wished they could go back.

The letters were still on the stone, a wish left ungranted.

"Oh," said Allie from behind him as Harding stared down at the stone in his hand, her voice suddenly choking off in disappointment. He watched the water run over the stone and his finger, rivulets spilling into the sink, crawling this way and that and glittering, and then he remembered. He lifted his face, looking at Allie in the mirror as she became the drowned ghost girl, her eyes rolling back and her hair soaking into rats' tail twists, and when the black water spilled from her mouth and spattered down her chin he screamed and screamed.

And then it was Halloween forever.

Why the Devil visited Martledge no one ever knew but visit he did, and not one time but many.

Of course, the first time he came no one knew it was Him because He came on a night of savage rain and bad-tempered wind, the sort that seems to want to find every gap and split in your clothing and to poke its deft fingers through those gaps and splits to tease and pinch your skin. It made the night a thing of stings and shivers so that the darkness seemed alive with malicious things, and from its centre came the Devil in the skin of a man. He walked out of the darkness along the Baby Way before turning and making His way into the town along a rambling, turnabout route that took Him first past the church and across the town green, along the back of the old smithy's forge and house, and in an almost complete loop around the brick factory. Few saw Him that first time because the weather had caused a swarm of closed curtains and firelight huddles and those that did saw little to alarm them. A man in a shabby suit, pale blue or grey, with a long black overcoat atop it flapping, bareheaded and wet.

No one shuddered at the sight of Him, and no babes woke shrieking from nightmares because He looked like a simple man caught in the rain but He was the Devil nonetheless, and it was 1919 and the world was wretched with flu and death.

After His long ramble around the town, He came to the Horse and Jockey public house. Martledge's other pub, the Green, had stayed closed but the Horse (as most people called it) was open. Robert Collier, the owner and landlord, had banked the fire low and lit only half the lanterns in anticipation of a quiet evening and so far he had been proved right, but it was a source of pride to him that he never stayed shut, no matter what the circumstances. Open he might be but he had no customers, not a soul, and so was busying himself wiping down the bar top and polishing the brass rails, buffing them to a glorious shine in which his face, curved and moon-eyed, stared back at him. When the door opened Robert Collier didn't look around but called, "Welcome! Enter as a friend, harm none here and leave as a valued companion," his standard greeting. Collis had muttonchops, wore a collarless white shirt under a black buttoned waistcoat, and looked and behaved every inch a landlord. He came from a long line of landlords, father and grandfather before him, and he was as proud of this lineage as any royal could be of theirs.

For a moment there was no movement and Collier turned to look at the fellow in the doorway. Medium height and build, clothes shabby and wet but clean, hair dark and face pale. Just a traveller in search of a drink, Collier thought, and repeated his greeting. Still the figure outside stayed motionless and Collier, looking on, had the strangest idea that the man was carefully weighing up the terms of his greeting and deciding whether to take the offer. Finally, He who Collis would come in a moment to understand was actually the Devil stepped into the Horse and Jockey. As he did so there was a flash like the spark of flint against flint, so quick as to be almost imaginary. Collier started, wondering if one of his lanterns had broken or if the fire had kicked out a woodknot, but then it was gone and the man was in the Horse.

Collier rose and took himself back behind the bar, saying to the him "And what'll you have on this terrible night, sir? Ale, or something stronger to keep the chill out?"

The man in the grey suit did not speak but simply nodded at Collis' best whiskey and Collier drew him a shot. As he turned to place the drink on the bar the man's image danced in the corner of his vision, in the part of sight that isn't really any use for seeing more than fragments and impressions, and what he glimpsed there was not a man. It wasn't anything he could name, nothing with edges or form, but was something both black and red and small and large, moving incessantly, shimmering, beautiful and old and clean and new and filthy and foul all at the same moment. It filled the whole of the snug bar and in its depths Collier saw reflected every awful, petty and mean thing he'd done and felt shame for them and felt every terrible thing that had been done to him being done again, all of life's embarrassments and slights happening at the same moment. He froze, helpless, drink held in mid-air, one foot off the floor, unable to move. *That's the Devil*, he thought, *come for me, come for me, oh God He's come for me.* The hand holding the drink shook slightly and the liquid within slopped up one edge of the glass, dangerously close to spilling and then Collier, without thinking, let the publican within him out, that professional veteran of nights handling drunks and days heaving barrels, the man who could stop arguments before they started with little more than a look.

"Sir, this is a fine drink," he said, and in speaking he was freed so could finish turning, placing the whiskey on the bar in front of the Devil. "You've chosen well. It'll warm you from the inside and keep the rain off." The Devil looked like a man again and He placed a coin on the bar for His drink. Collier took it and put it in his pocket without looking at it.

"It's a terrible night," said Collier, now all professional ale man and not frightened because he had remembered that the Devil had agreed his terms before entering his establishment. The Devil nodded and swallowed his drink then gestured up at the top shelf of the spirits for another. Collis turned and reached for the same bottle, ignoring the thing that was again writhing in the corner of his eye, and saw that there was a bottle he'd not seen before in amongst all the others. It was dark green and the label on it had a picture of some place that Collis wanted never to visit, although he couldn't say why. He took the bottle, which felt warm and dry and itched against his skin, and turned back to the Devil. When he uncorked it, the bottle released an odour of peat and smoke and fire and ash, and when he poured it out it was the colour of amber with sparks at its heart of red and black. The Devil took his drink and indicated that Collier should have one with him, still not speaking.

Collier poured a drink from the Devil's bottle and sipped at it, trying not to think of deals sealed at crossroads at midnight and shillings found at the bottom of pint glasses awash in puddles of foam. He had made no deal, after all, or at least if he had he was the instigator of it, not some beneficial signatory.

The liquid tasted like it smelled, the sharpest and driest whiskey Collis had ever had the fortune to try. It drew his lips back across his teeth as though strings were pulling at the corners of his mouth so sharp was it, and the saliva in his mouth near curdled in sympathy with it. He should add water but that would be a crime against this fine, fine drink. It went to his head in a way no other whiskey had, made him feel hot and somehow inviolate.

The Devil put two more coins on the bar, put his glass down and turned to go. Collier, emboldened, said, "Come again, sir! You'll always be welcome if you come as friend."

"A year, then," said the Devil, almost the only words He ever spoke in Martledge, and then He took His leave. Collier watched Him walk up the road until the rain and the wind and the dark swallowed Him and only then did he allow himself to relax and become Collier the small, mortal man again, hot with whiskey and the triumph of what he had done.

The next day word was all over Martledge that the Devil had visited the Horse and Jockey, not just visited but drunk there as well. By evening the Horse was full and doing a roaring trade, and Collier was regaling all there with the story about how he had served the Devil and, indeed, drunk with Him. People inspected the floor where the Devil's foot had first landed and made the flash and found that there was a mark on the flag, not of a cloven hoof but of a bare human foot with long, thin toes. The mark seemed to confirm a long-held rumour, that the Horse's original owner, Jack Collier (grandfather of the current landlord), had stolen stone intended for the repair of the church to create the Horse's fine flagged floor, for why else would the Devil's foot react to it and leave a mark if not for the fact the stone was, at some level, sacred?

There was much gossip around Collier's story, and many questions, all of which Collier answered honestly and fairly. Yes, he had served the Devil two drinks and taken a single drink with Him, Yes he had known it was the Devil almost immediately (which was almost the truth, almost if not exactly) and no, he had felt no fear (almost the truth, so close to the truth as to make no difference). People listened and marvelled, and they bought drinks, and the Horse was a place of jollity and warmth and community.

And then the priest came in.

Father Marten was accompanied by his verger, John. Lollylolly and Nodding John they were called behind their backs, because when Father Marten gave a sermon he could go on for what felt like hours until, by the end, it felt as though all you were hearing was a constant repeating word *lollylollylollylolly*, while John stood at his side nodding enthusiastically. A path to the bar cleared for them without anyone apparently moving and the two men came and stood in front of Collier.

"Father," said Collier, amiably enough. He was not a churchgoer and had never suffered through one of his interminable sermons, so he still liked the priest.

"I'll take a whiskey, please, Robert," said Lollylolly, but didn't order a drink for Nodding John. Collier drew the priest's drink and passed it over the bar.

"Is this not from the special bottle, then, Robert?"

So, thought Collier, it was to be that kind of meeting.

"No, Father. I'm saving that for next year in case He visits again."

"'He', Robert Collier? 'He'? The Devil you mean?"

"I suppose I do, Father."

"Ah, Robert. Have you thought about this? Truly thought?"

"There's not much to think about, Father. He comes and He buys his drinks fairly, or He does not come. There's all there is to it."

"Really? Have you no shame, Robert, no shame at all? Giving succour and shelter to that abomination? The next time He comes, Robert Collier, if He should dare to come again, you send Him away and deny Him entry, do you hear?" Marten sipped his whiskey and made a face. Collier had drawn him only a cheap blend rather than one of the single malts.

"Do I hear you, Father?" said Collier. He bristled, unable to help himself. He had spent the last few years of his life in muddy trenches with the air about him full of flying metal that might tear him apart at any second, following sometimes contradictory orders given by fools, and his time for being told what to do was, he had decided the moment he returned from France, over. "I hear you, but I'll do no such thing."

"What?" said Lollylolly.

"I believe you heard, Father."

"You refuse? Think, man, think! You cannot allow the Devil into your place of business and think you can keep yourself safe from him. Think, for the love of God, think! No good will come of this."

"I have thought, Father, and do you know what I think? I think you should be thanking me, not criticising me."

"What?" Now the priest seemed thunderstruck and near-wordless. Nodding John was no longer nodding.

"That's right, thanking me. The Devil came and supped here but He did no harm because He stuck to my rules. He entered as a friend and left as a companion and did no evil whilst here. I tamed the Devil, Father, I *bound* Him, and for a time He did no wrong in the world. Surely that's reason for thanks rather than talking to me like I'm a surly child in Sunday School?"

"'Tamed the Devil'? The arrogance of you, Robert Collier, the very *arrogance!* To think you can best the great deceiver, the great enemy, and worse that you seem to be proud of it! Perhaps the Devil came here to make you proud, Collier, did you consider that? That this pride has been made in you by Him to make you sin?"

Actually, Collier had considered this and had dismissed it as a nonsense. It wasn't a reckless pride he felt but a reasonable one, for surely it was acceptable to be proud of facing down the Devil himself? "If I'm such a prideful man, Father, you'd best leave my establishment and take your servant with you," said Collier.

Father Marten swallowed the last of his drink and turned to go, but then turned back as though something had struck him. "Tell me, did the Devil pay you? And did you keep his coin?"

"He did and I did. There are three of them, Father, which is three more than you've given me for your drink and might tell us something about the Devil compared to local priests, don't you think?" Collier had the coins in his pocket now, although he was damned if he'd tell the priest that. Each of them was old, stamped with writing on that he could not read. Two had heads of people he did not recognise, one a picture that might have been an animal or plant, it was impossible to tell.

By now the pub was silent, everyone listening to the argument.

"Robert, my friend, will you not reconsider," said Lollylolly as calmly as a man under great strain could. "You are embracing the sin of pride and coming dangerously close to blasphemy. Will you repent and be blessed? For the sake of your immortal soul?"

"No, Father, I will not," said Collier, and that was that.

~

The next months were lean for the Horse, and for Collier. People might not have liked Lollylolly's sermons but he was still their priest, and much as they might even have agreed with Collier's stance they wouldn't go against God's vessel in Martledge. Few of them came to the pub and his takings were low, and he found himself surviving on the patronage of three or four of the local naysayers and rabblerousers and the meagre savings his father had left at the time of his death. Memories are long in Martledge, and while Lollylolly and Nodding John had stopped referring to the Devil's visit, people still gossiped about it. Of course, in gossip it grew and by the time the year's anniversary of the visit came around people had Collier kissing the Devil's feet and throwing Lollylolly and Nodding John from the pub in a fit of fury, all the while praising the Devil and insulting God.

Collier, too proud and too convinced of his own rightness in this affair, would do nothing to ease the tensions. No apology passed his lips and no sign did he show of feeling anything other than justified. "I fought in the war to have this freedom," he would say if pushed on the matter, "and no priest nor Devil nor man will tell me how to run my life or my business, and I'll serve who I want as long as they stick to my rules because I am a landlord to all if they pay and behave."

A year to the day after the Devil first came to Martledge, He came again.

Father Marten had, in the strictest terms, forbidden his flock to leave their homes that night, citing the risk from "the things that might walk abroad" rather than mentioning Collier or the pub or the Devil specifically, and Collier had, in a rare display of sensitivity, put a sign up on the Horse's door saying that it would be 'Closed to the Public' that night. Still, he lit the lamps and stoked the fire to warmth and unlocked his door at the usual time.

The Devil entered Martledge from the other side of town this time, walking along the path through The Meadows by the river. People might not have been allowed out but they crowded their parlours and watched through their windows as he passed, a small man in a pale grey suit. The weather was better this year, the air warmer and dry, and he wore no overcoat. Some people were disappointed in how he looked, expecting the Great Adversary to be all horns and goat-headed horrors, and wondered if this were not some grand hoax conjured up by Collier, but those who caught the Devil in the corners of their vision and saw the shape beneath the shape knew he was as real as the world beneath their feet. Children cried at the sight of him and adults waited until he had passed and tried to pretend that their fear wasn't making their bodies shake and shudder and clutched at crosses and bibles for comfort.

Collier had a drink from the Devil's bottle poured ready.

He had not presumed to pour himself one and this year the Devil did not offer, simply collecting His drink and taking it to the booth in the corner. He sat, sipping at his whiskey, and when He had finished He raised a finger for another, which Collier poured and took over. There were two coins on the table which Collier lifted and placed in his pocket, feeling obscurely disappointed that he had not been permitted to sup with the Devil this year. It felt like a demotion, a slight. When the Devil rose to leave, Collier asked, "Next year?" and the Devil simply nodded.

And so it went.

People started to frequent the Horse again as new scandals took their attentions, and Collier's profits rose and the pressures on him lessened. Each year the Devil would visit, Lollylolly would instruct people to not even look at him but they would hide at the corners of their windows and stare anyway, and each year Collier would close the Horse except for his single customer. Some years the Devil would buy Collier a drink, others not; but Collier served him faithfully, always calling "Welcome! Enter as a friend, harm none here and leave as a valued companion," when the Devil arrived but before He had stepped inside, and always the Devil paused as though weighing up His options before making His decision and stepping in.

During these years Collier found a woman prepared to put up with him and they married and they had a son. They grew older together, the landlord's muttonchops whitening and his waistcoats going up in size as his belly expanded, his child reaching his teen years and then adulthood and leaving home to make his own fortune. Lollylolly said no more in public about the Devil except for his yearly exhortation to stay home, but he never set foot in the Horse and Jockey again. Nodding John, for his part, would sometimes go in and take a drink of an evening but he always made sure he paid for what he took and he never entered wearing his robes. Eventually, people became accustomed to the Devil's visits and they became a thing like any other. Martledge grew around them like flesh around an old splinter until they were buried deep and bothered hardly anyone.

What only two men in Martledge knew was that each year, on the morning of the Devil's visit, from the second visit onwards, Collier would find a handwritten note pushed under the door of the Horse. Each was the same, always reading:

Robert
> *I beg you to reconsider this for the sake of your soul.*
> *Your friend*
> *Lollylolly*

It was only after receiving several of these that Collier realised the priest had signed with the nickname the townsfolk used behind his back rather than the more formal *Father Marten*.

After many years Lollylolly retired and a new priest, Father Daniels, took his place. Before he left, Lollylolly explained about the Devil's visits and shortly thereafter Father Daniels had a private meeting with Collier. The meeting was, by both men's accounts, amiable and afterwards the men would greet each other on the street as happy acquaintances although Collier still did not go to church and Daniels did not frequent the Horse to drink. Daniels also left a note each year for Collier, always the same wording, although his were signed *Father Daniels*.

The Devil's bottle remained on the shelf with the rest of the spirits, its label offering no hint as to the liquid within. Collier refused to serve anyone from it despite numerous requests, and never touched it except for when the Devil called. The level of liquid in it never seemed to fall in spite of the drinks poured from it.

The night of the Devil's last visit the weather was the same as the night of his first. Rain squalled and swirled and the wind flapped the Devil's coat behind Him as He walked Martledge's streets. People no longer bothered to look out of their windows as the Devil passed, and the younger generations didn't know he visited at all, or if they had been told He did they thought the stories were simply a myth. Father Daniels spent the night in St Clements, praying. He was not scared and wasn't even sure he believed in the visits but he had left the note as Father Marten had asked him to do and prayed in case, also as Marten had asked him to do, the wind hopefully carrying his prayers to God's ears on their gusts.

Collier waited and greeted the Devil as he always did when he arrived.

That night the Devil bought Collier a drink, paying for His own two and Collier's one with three coins as He always did. Instead of leaving after His drinks, however, he came to the bar and for the first time leaned towards Collier and beckoned him close. Collier, suddenly nervous, leaned in and for a moment he was close to the Devil, seeing him both in front and from the side, both sides of Him at once, the man and the terrible, shifting thing that he had no words to describe and it was like having his head split in two and he wanted to scream out but daren't as the Devil's lips, if that's what they were, were brushing his ear. Quietly, almost inaudibly, the Devil spoke to Collier, saying the second and last thing he would speak aloud in the Horse and Jockey.

Then, as Collier watched, the Devil left the Horse and Jockey, stepping over His own print from years before and out into the wild weather beyond the door. Collier thought about what the Devil had said to him and looked at the darkness through the still-open door and saw the rain and it was as though the sky itself was crying for him and truly, he wanted to cry for himself, but he could not as his tears had dried and were like sad dust in his eyes.

Collier never told anyone what the Devil said to him but he was not the same after that last visit, quieter and more subdued, nervous, starting at shadows. He smiled little and no longer laughed, and he never greeted new arrivals at the Horse and Jockey except with a simple "Hello" or, more often, a curt nod. The Devil's bottle was gone from the spirits shelf.

Collier died three months later and Martledge mourned him appropriately and then returned to normal, grief put aside until the next passing. Collier's son, like his father in looks and temperament, came home to run the Horse and the Devil never visited the town again so far as anyone knew.

A month or so after Collier's death, Lollylolly received a parcel from the old landlord's solicitor. When he opened it, he found a note and, carefully wrapped in a twist of velvet, a roll of coins, all old and none of which he recognised. He read the note, which was brief, and then looked at the coins again but did not touch them. *Ah, Robert,* thought Lollylolly, letting the note fall to the floor where it lay at his feet. A tear rolled down his cheek as he twisted the coins back into the velvet, still without touching them. *Ah Robert, I tried so hard.*

The note said simply,

I took them but I never spent or sold or gave away a single one of them. You were right and he was not my friend nor worthy of my trust. I should, I see now, have listened to you. Thank you for your friendship even if I spurned it all these years.

Your friend, Robert Collier.

The note was addressed not to Lollylolly but, more formally, to *Father Marten*.

The Fools' Parade

They came down from the hills that day, as we knew they would. With the mist curling between their legs they seemed strangely eldritch, as though they were floating rather than walking, skipping, somersaulting and running. By appearing, they made another link in a chain of tradition that had run so long it had become both Law and Given. No one in the three Villages knows truly when or how the Fools' Parade was first performed, but it has occurred as part of our traditions as long as our spoken records and campfire stories go back. Every first of April they would come: the capering idiots, the jugglers, the acrobats, every sort of clown imaginable. All the types of figures of fun and merriment that exist would walk the roads that link the three Villages and form the Triangle.

My own earliest recollection of the Fools' Parade is a happy one. I was three or four years old and was just beginning to understand the idea that whilst there might not be any human habitations for miles around the Triangle, there was definitely another world stretching out there past the farms and houses that I knew, and I had started to wonder what that world might look like, what it might smell and taste and feel like. One day, I was woken early. This, in itself, was not unusual, but the fact that it was my father who woke me was, as he normally left to work in the fields long before sunrise and even longer before I arose. It became clear to me very quickly that this was to be a strange day and that something unusual was going to happen.

Overnight, brightly coloured flags had grown from the roofs of the houses like some glorious fungi and the roads were lined with tables, belly-bent with food and drink. My father, a usually taciturn and calm man, seemed ill at ease and talked constantly with my mother, my older sister and me. I had never heard such a stream of words from his mouth before, and I delighted in it. Finally, we had father's attention and it was such an unexpected thing that it was like holding a snowflake, marvelling at it but desperate for it not to melt.

Father bade us hurry our dressing, told us again and again to be quick and not to dally, helped us with our clothes and encouraged us not to dawdle. Adelaine, my sister, was excited as well, but would not tell me why. When I looked out of my bedroom window, the streets (street, really, as our village is the smallest of the three in the Triangle and is really only a cluster of homes and farms huddled around a large track) were not only full of tables and food and drink, but also people. Whole families, all dressed in their neatest clothes, were standing near the tables and talking good-humouredly. Children, some of them my friends and some Adelaine's, were chasing between their parents and somewhere nearby music was playing, a guitar and mandolin and a violin.

Once my sister and I had our best clothes on (and had done our complaining about stiff shoes and itchy collars), the family went outside to join the ever-growing crowd. It felt like the whole village was present lining the street, and that everyone was laughing, talking and having a good time. I asked my father what was happening, and he replied – and I remember his answer well because when I was older, I realised that it was one of his rare witticisms – "Hilarity on the hoof, son. Jokes at the speed of a slow man's walk." My mother, who I think never really liked my father much, told him to shush, and then said to me, "'Tis the Fools' Parade", as though this would explain everything. It did not, of course, being as cryptic to me as the answer that my father had given. My mother was, I believe, a somewhat stupid woman who lived her life knowing that the man that she had married was a great deal cleverer than her and resented him for it, but no matter. That's not the point of this telling.

That first time for me was a revelation. The Parade came out of the hills, as it was to do on every occasion after and had done on every occasion previously. There was, and is, no real order to it, just a long line of acrobats, showmen and clowns. I distinctly remember two clowns, one falling and tumbling and the other telling loud off-colour jokes, being next to each other in the ever-moving line of Fools, and them being followed by a ballerina wearing the mask of a pig. Their acts clashed entirely but to a young child it didn't matter. It did not seem to matter to the adults watching either. As they walked, the Fools took what food and drink they wanted off the tables, but they never stopped walking or performing, a continual line of men and women and children in makeup and strange clothes, drifting through our Village. I felt strangely proud that we should be so blessed, and I have a feeling that most of the other children felt the same way.

Eventually, the line of Fools tailed off, the gaps between the prancing figures becoming larger and larger until there were none to come. There was no sense of show or drama to this ending, and I felt disappointed that the day's entertainment was over. However, I was wrong. To my surprise, the villagers began to fall in line behind the procession of Fools and follow them. My family joined the line as well, and I was hoisted aloft onto Father's shoulders so that I could see. The line stretched out for nearly as far as the eye could see, and it was obvious that it was heading towards the next Village. The procession's movement was easy and relaxed, a constant speed was held and people took what refreshments they wanted off tables as they passed. I was passed a pie and munched it cheerily as we made our way onwards.

Through that bright spring morning we walked. We passed through the next Village and went sedately on to the largest of the Villages that make up the Triangle. Here, the Fools' Parade finally stopped, and the villagers stopped with it. In the main square, easily big enough to hold all the inhabitants of the three Villages and all the performers, the Fools finally gave us their show. Each Fool claimed an area of the square for him- or herself and performed. Some tumbled, some juggled, some joked and some sang. Some danced. One played a violin deliberately badly, and changed the lyrics of the tunes he sang to ribald, bawdy tales that my mother dragged me away from hearing. The square became a riot of moving colour and twisting, melting noise.

Now fully released, children ran among the adults and the adults talked and drank, laughing at the things they saw and heard, and so it continued all day, with people eating and drinking and being friendlier to each other than I had seen before.

At dusk, the Fools left quietly, slipping out from the square in a ragged line and heading off into the hills. I thought that this might mean the end of the day's festivities, but it was not so. People continued as though the Fools had never left or, more accurately, as though they had never been there. Even that young, I realised that this was an unusual way for people to behave. I saw Father, deep in a drunken conversation with a man I knew he did not like. Where normally Father would not give this man the time of day, they were now amiably discussing something as though they were lifelong friends. I saw my sister being chased by a boy I did not think she knew and kissing him when he caught her. It was all very confusing.

Sometime later in the evening, when night had fallen properly, lanterns were lit all over the square and the orange flickering light they cast made everything seem distant and detached. The lighting of the lanterns apparently also acted as a signal, and the Fools came back. They came back still in line, but no longer performing. To my eyes they still looked imbued with a sense of fun and amusement, but the adults fell silent at their reappearance and the atmosphere became tense. The square was more silent than I had ever experienced before, except for the squeals of the still-playing children and the frantic hushing noises of their parents. Eventually, all the children were quiet too. The Fools stepped into the silence, walking around the square on gentle feet. They moved slowly, here splitting away from the Parade in twos and threes, there joining the column again. Still no one spoke.

After several minutes of this, I became bored, but my father's hand clamped firmly on my shoulder prevented me from roaming as I had done earlier. This strange part of the Parade lasted for a long time, further into the night than I had stayed awake before, with Fools constantly breaking off and being reabsorbed into the column which all the while moved around the edge of the square. My legs had begun to ache and my eyes felt heavy, when the Fools finally stopped. Two Fools left the column and walked slowly around the square, circling the Villagers who stood motionless and quiet in the dark. Eventually, the two Fools stopped in front of the elder of the two doctors who served the Triangle, and began to gently pluck at his sleeve. The doctor turned to his wife, kissed her quickly and then let the two Fools lead him away. The Parade began again as it had when I first saw it, with all the participants performing their acts, but this time there was a difference, because as the Parade left the square, the doctor walked with them. I saw his wife crying, standing in the centre of a circle of people that had formed around her as the Villagers moved slowly away from her. I could not understand for the life of me what was so bad. It seemed to me that to be taken with the Fools was a great privilege. I could not see why the doctor's wife was so upset – surely the Doctor was to have a fabulous time with all those Dancers and Clowns and Acrobats? Maybe she was crying for joy. I did not realise it then, but no one would ever see the doctor again.

It was only later that I found out the significance of the last part of the Fools' Parade. Each year, the Fools would decide amongst themselves which inhabitant of the Triangle had been the most foolish or stupid or negligent, and then they took them away. Each year as I grew older, I would look for the people taken in previous years, but I never did see one. They were simply gone. The Fools came as ever but there were no new Fools amongst them, no familiar faces to be recognised as one of our old neighbours.

I am a man now. I have a family of my own, a wife and two children and responsibilities that I could not even dream of when I was a child. The Fools' parade has been one of many constants in my life, occurring year in, year out. Thirteen years after I first remember seeing the Fools' Parade, the person the Fools took was my father. They did so, everyone assumed, because he had chosen to send my brother (born when I was nine) outside of the Triangle to be educated. It was something of a shock when my father did this – no one had ever thought that he held ideas that were even the slightest part revolutionary. By the time the parade came, everyone was certain who was to be taken, and everyone was right. My father went without a struggle (as everyone I have ever seen has done), merely kissing my mother and hugging my sister and me. Although I was seventeen at the time, and trying to be a man, I cried and cried as he left. I remember very clearly that it was below freezing that night, and my father's breath frosted before him as he walked away. Dignified and calm, he went to a fate that still remains unknown.

Surprising though my father's actions might have been to most, I did not find them odd at all. I had heard enough comments from him, muttered asides and passing phrases over the years to alert me to the fact that he was deeply unhappy with the insular, unchanging life of the Triangle. He wanted to progress, to make life better, and I think he realised that if it was too late for his existence to improve, that his children and their children may yet feel some benefit. I was already deep into my schooling and life in the Triangle by the time he resolved to act upon his thoughts, but my brother was just the right age. I think that Father hoped that he might somehow get away with what he'd done. Certainly, he wanted his actions to have no consequences for Michael, who had been too young to take part in any decision-making processes about his own future. And so my father was taken, and my brother was educated.

I do not know if it was my father's intention or not, but my brother came back, found that my father had been taken and started to ask questions. He asked about the right of the Fools to make decisions for the Triangle, why things did not change and who had given the Fools permission to act in this way in the first place. More importantly, he began to teach the Villagers about how things happened in other parts of the world, how everyone had a vote and how change was positively encouraged. In the months leading up to this year's Fools' Parade, there were no doubts about who was to be taken. My brother was the one and only candidate, and although the Fools had made some unusual or unexpected choices in the past, no one could see them doing that this time. Michael would walk out of the Village with the Fools, everyone knew, and there was no one who could or would change this fact.

No one, that is, except my brother himself. The most important thing that my brother did this year occurred a few days before the Parade was due to take place. He disappeared. Rather than let the Fools have any sort of control over him, he simply left, and he has not come back since. Unlike the loss of my father, the absence of my brother is tinged with victory for me. I am sure he is alive somewhere, just as I am sure that my father is dead.

The morning of April the First this year was grey and overcast. The Fools appeared, as they always did, like some fae phenomena given life and physical presence for just one day, but this year the day also confirmed something for me. The adults may turn it into a great celebration and the children may get a day to run and play with their friends, but this merely covers the true feelings involved. The adults are *terrified*. They're terrified of being taken and they're terrified of being chosen and they're terrified of the Fools. The older I get, the more frightened I become. I am comfortable in the life I have made myself, and while the thought of dying doesn't bother me, the idea of missing out on the time I might have with my wife and children fills me with a kind of primal, gut-twisting fear. I cannot lose them, these people I love, and so I have toed the line and I kept my head down and remained as unnoticed as I can. I think that this is the power that the Fools have over us.

I still do not know where the Fools go in the period between each Parade, nor do I care. Scared as I am of them, I am rapidly coming to the opinion that my father and brother might be right, that we cannot allow Fools to make our decisions for us. I have a dream sometimes that my father is somewhere up in the hills surrounding the Triangle, living in a position of authority in the Fools' own village, but I do not see how this can be. I am sure he is dead, killed not because he was foolish, but because he was sensible and tried to do something intelligent and wise. Those places my brother spoke of seem to have a much better system for governing their lives than we in the Triangle do, and I think that the Fools know it. The Fools' parade returns here still, year after year, but I hope it can only be a matter of time until the Triangle sees that we cannot allow the Fools to still have their Parade and make our decisions for us.

They are, after all, only Fools.

Mallory had popped into O'Dowd's on the way back from work so that the inevitable argument that would occur at home with Marie was at least postponed, ignoring the fact that the argument would almost certainly start with his having popped into O'Dowd's.

Mallory liked O'Dowd's. He liked that it was dark, that it smelled of old beer and cleaning fluid and whiskey, that it didn't serve food except for small packets of nuts. The people who went into O'Dowd's weren't there to socialise or be gregarious and make noise, and they certainly weren't there to find answers. They were there, he was sure, to forget the questions. George, the surly tattooed barman, set Mallory's drink in front of him, expertly poured as ever and the glass cold and frosted with condensation, and then left him alone. The only words George ever spoke were to ask what drink you wanted and to tell you your bill, and once he knew what you ordered he stopped doing even that. He had a tattoo of a snake on his inner forearm and sometimes, when his muscles tensed, it looked like the snake was peering around as though to check that everyone was still respecting O'Dowd's downbeat, melancholy atmosphere.

Mallory took his phone out, debating messaging Marie. She'd know, of course, by his absence that he'd popped somewhere on his way back from work so why, he thought, tell her? Why open the can of worms any earlier than he absolutely had to? He put the phone on the bar, screen down, and took a long swallow of his drink. Surly and tattooed he might be, but George could pour a perfect drink, Mallory had to give him that. When he put the drink down, his fingers leaving ghosts of themselves in the misting of liquid on the glass, he was surprised to find a man sitting on the seat along from him.

The man was dressed well, in an expensive jacket and what looked like brand-name jeans and good quality shoes, but his hair was wild, as though he'd been walking in a high wind. Was it windy outside? It hadn't been when Mallory entered, it had been mild and sunny. George approached the man, who ordered a double shot of one of O'Dowd's higher-end whiskeys, paying with a new, uncreased bill. When George had retreated back along the bar to his stool under the always-dark television screen, the man turned to Mallory and said, "Where am I?"

Turning to face him, Mallory could see something like madness in the man's eyes, which were slightly frantic, red-rimmed and wider than looked comfortable. He half-expected them to roll in their sockets like those of a panicking horse.

"Please," the man said, "tell me where I am." His voice was low, polite, and fringed with something that might have been despair or might have been something far, far worse. Mallory instinctively pushed his stool back from the man and said, in the calmest voice he could manage, "You're in O'Dowds. It's on Rackham Street near the bus station. Are you lost?"

"Lost? Sort of. More like unfound. Untethered, maybe," the man replied and drained his glass in one go, raising it to George after to indicate another. He nodded at Mallory's glass as well and Mallory suddenly decided that the man maybe wasn't so bad. First impressions could, after all, be misleading. George put their drinks down and took the man's money and went away and the man said, "Rackham Street? Okay, that's fine, that's not too far. I was going to the bank I think. I went to the bank. I have money so I must have. But then I was here. It's happening more and more."

"What is?" asked Mallory draining his own drink and moving on to the one the man had bought him.

"It doesn't have a name because it's never happened to anyone but me and I'm not big on labels, not really. It's just what's happening." Listening, Mallory had a sudden sense that the man was far from home, not just miles but years, *aeons* away, that he was as lost a man as Mallory had ever met and it made him feel awfully, desperately sad. Without thinking, he picking up his phone and texted Marie, *I won't be long. I love you xx*. He never usually said it, never put kisses on his texts, hadn't since the raw and troubled times had begun between them a few months ago, but now it seemed important. It seemed vital. Moments later her reply appeared, as though she'd been waiting for him to message: *Where are you?*

He debated lying but didn't and sent, *O'Dowd's. I won't be long and I won't be drunk when I get back. I promise. Maybe we can spend some time together tonight? xx*

Marie's reply was a simple *OK xx* and he saw the kisses, noticeably absent from her recent communications as well, and thought that maybe there was hope after all.

"Hey, you're not infectious are you?" asked Mallory as what the man had said sunk in, moving further away. The man gave a low, sad laugh and said, "Infected maybe, but not infectious. You're safe sitting by me."

"Infected with what?" Mallory asked, relaxing a little although still remaining wary.

"I told you, I haven't given it a name," and the man sounded testy now, tired and stressed and approaching some kind of snapping point. He drained his second drink and ordered a third. He gestured again but Mallory shook his head, remembering what he'd said to Marie. "I suppose you might call it Mamdani's disease but maybe you wouldn't. I don't really understand it, to be honest. I just know it's here, and it's in me."

"Mamdani?" asked Mallory as George put the man's next drink down. There was a strange blurring motion and then the glass was in the man's hand, raised halfway to his lips. Mallory blinked. He hadn't seen the man's arm move. He hadn't seen the glass move. George didn't appear to notice anything but the man did. He paused the drink, holding it motionless for a few seconds and then said, "Again," and swallowed it in another single tilt.

"Did..." Mallory began before trailing off, because how could you ask that? *Did you just pick up that drink without moving?* The man grinned at him and said, as though Mallory had asked the question out loud, "I did. You saw?"

"Yes, but I don't know what I saw. A trick, I assume?"

"No. Not a trick, or at least not one I played on you. Maybe a trick the universe played on me and you're the audience for it this time. I don't know."

"You're not making sense," said Mallory, trying not to get irritated. He wanted to get away now, to walk through a doorway that had opened, maybe just a crack but opened nonetheless, and to find a way back home with Marie, a way back to the people they had been when they first met. To the people who'd laughed.

"I'm sorry," said the man, sounding genuinely contrite. "I'll try and explain but it won't make any sense, not really."

"Won't it?"

"Fuck, no," said the man, and this time his grin looked like the last wolfish symptom of a sickness, long festering and ravenously hungry. "I mean, I can say it, but sense? No. I've left that far behind.

"To begin I need to tell you a little about me. About what I do. It is relevant, I promise. Just bear with me. So, I work for a small team of engineers and scientists and we all who work for a company that sells itself to whichever company can pay them the most. We look at new car designs and try to improve them before they go to manufacture and market."

"You're a scientist?"

"God no, not me. I haven't the mind for it. I'm a driver. I see if things work in reality that have previously only been tested in the computer. I'm sorry, I'm not being clear. Hold on." The man took a deep breath, steadying himself, and swept his hands back through his hair, dragging it into some semblance of control. "Let's say my colleagues come up with tweaks to the engine or body shape that they think will make the car more efficient. It gets tested in computer models first and then the original design is also run through the models to get baseline figures, an idea of what improvements have been made. The original design car is then road tested under various driving conditions to get real world figures which can be compared to the computer model ones. You see?"

"Yeah. Makes sense," said Mallory although he was floundering a little. Cars? Models? What had this to do with the man's illness?

"After that a version of the car is made incorporating the design tweaks and it's also road tested using exactly the same tests as the original car underwent, to see if those computer models are accurate, and if its performance or speed or fuel consumption or whatever has improved over the original design version. Well, that's where I come in. I drive the cars.

"We have a one mile track and it can be made wet, slippy, I can go at speed or go slow, skid, whatever. I'm a good driver, an excellent one really, and I can do the same manoeuvre in the two cars as closely as possible so that the comparisons are accurate. And that's what I do. I run cars around a track making them do whatever tasks I'm told, and until recently it was a great life."

"So what happened?" and Mallory suddenly didn't want to know the answer, because the answer felt like it might be something serious, too serious, and he just wanted to find a way out, to get back to something he thought had been lost perhaps for ever, but the man trapped him by saying, "One of the others had an idea.

"It was quite simple really. Lorenz came in one morning to the storming sessions we had every day and said he'd had a thought. I should say, the project we were working on was a relaunch, an older model car that had been updated several times and was a flagship release for the company. One of the things they were keen on was for the newer models to have the best gas mileage, or electric charge mileage, and that's what we were working on. We'd looked at things like photovoltaic panels to boost the battery charge and I'd been looking at how the car ran, trying to tweak its engine efficiency. Nothing unusual really. We never made huge leaps, those had already happened before the designs reached us, we just made what was already there as good as possible. An extra mile per gallon here, a saving of a few cents or euros or pounds there.

"So anyway, Lorenz says he's had a thought and we all wait and he says, 'Fuzzy logic' and we all stare and he says again, 'Fuzzy logic'. And Janey, she's the team lead and she's not the most patient of people or the most forgiving says, 'What the fuck?' and someone else says 'I don't understand' and I remember thinking I didn't even know what fuzzy logic was.

"'Hear me out,' says Lorenz. 'We've been approaching this like a Boolian logic problem with either a yes or no solution – we can definitely make the car run better or we can't – but there's another way to see it, isn't there?'

"'Another way?' says Janey. "Another way to what? A journey of ten miles is a journey of ten miles, it uses the same amount of gas or charge, that's non-negotiable. If I drive ten miles at ten miles an hour twice then the same energy is used on each occasion, and I travel the same distance and it takes me the same length of time.'

"'Yes,' says Lorenz and he's smiling wide like he's been given all the gifts on Christmas morning and he's about to share them, 'but what if the journey wasn't ten miles? What if it was only nine? Then the energy usage would be less, and so would the time taken.'

"'And you'd still be a mile from the shops,' said Janey and she sounded disgusted, like Lorenz had suggested we have an orgy, or puked on the table or something."

The man took another swallow of his drink, and when had George brought him that? Mallory hadn't seen it happen but there it was, a new double in front of the man.

"Anyway, Lorenz just keeps smiling. 'Have you ever noticed how the same journey can seem longer or shorter depending on the day or your mood? Sometimes it'll seem like it takes a moment, sometimes the same thing takes *forever*, yes?' and we all nodded because we all knew that feeling, and Lorenz said, 'That's fuzzy logic. What is it they say? In additional to the yes and the no, the universe contains a maybe? Well, what if we exploit the maybe?'

"'Ten miles is ten miles,' says Janey and her voice is past pedantic now and into boss mode. We'd all had it aimed at us at one time or another, her temper and her will and her 'do it my way or else' speech, and now it looked like it was Lorenz' turn.

"'Until it isn't,' said Lorenz and he was maddeningly calm. 'Look, let's not argue. I think we can persuade the car that the journey is shorter using fuzzy logic algorithms so that on a ten mile journey it's only travelled eight or nine and we'll make an energy and a time saving. Let's add the programming to the on-board systems and see what happens?'

"'Surely if we see any reduced journey distances that'll simply indicate that the on-board systems are incorrect, not that's there's been any actual reduction in distance travelled or fuel used or the time taken!' says Janey, and she's not calm, not at all now."

The man looked at his now empty glass, seemed to be having some kind of internal debate, and then put it back on the counter without motioning to George. Feeling like he should try and contribute Mallory said, "Do you want another? My shout?"

"No, thank you," said the man. "Anyway, Lorenz wouldn't let it go. 'What's it going to hurt?' he kept asking and then he'd smile that maddening grin and eventually Janey said, 'Well, just do it then but when it doesn't work I'll expect an apology in front of everyone.'

"'Fair enough,' says Lorenz and then says to me, 'We know exactly how long the track is, yes?'

"'We do,' I say. 'If I hold the centre line it's exactly one mile. Here's a question though. Assuming we add fuzzy logic programming to the on-board travel computer and it tells us that the journey is shorter than we think it should be, how can you tell if it's an actual reduction and not just like Janey says, a glitch?'

"'Easy,' says Lorenz and he's clearly been thinking about it, 'we add separate physical odometers to each wheel. We run the car without the fuzzy logic switched on so we've got five separate recordings of distance, four wheels and the engine computer, to ensure we have a match, and then we turn on the fuzzy logic. If all four wheels record the same reduction as the computer system, it's worked. If they don't, well then I'm apologising to everyone.'

"'And buying the first round in the bar,' added Janey and she doesn't sound as angry now, just a little smug, like she'd got her own way.

"After that, the discussion went back to something about foils and counterfoils and I kind of tuned out. Unless the issues being discussed were mechanical or to do with driving improvements I tended not to have much to input. Anyway, we were starting practical testing the next day and that was always more fun that the talkie stuff."

The man sighed deeply and lifted his now empty glass. Mallory lifted a finger to George who came over and refilled it and then went to refill Mallory's. Mallory, to his genuine surprise, shook his head. He glanced at his phone and saw another message from Marie, a single '?'. As the man drained his new drink Mallory typed a quick reply, *Still here but not drinking will explain when back love you xx*, knowing as he sent it that it sounded lame, like an excuse arrived at on the hoof and without depth or structure. Marie must have been sitting on her phone though because a reply arrived straight away, *Okay xx* and look, there were kisses and Mallory felt again a yearning to be back with her because these openings, this opening, felt small and limited and at risk of disappearing and he desperately, clutchingly didn't want that because he didn't know when, or if, another would present itself.

"Anyway, next day we started trialling the various amendments. There was stuff about fuel lines, a change to the power management system, various small things and by the time we'd finished for the day we'd increased the mpg by a small amount. Nothing much, but in a tight marker everything helps, you know?"

"Yes," said Mallory, not really knowing.

"Next day, we were ready for Lorenz' ideas to be tested. First, we ran the car around the track, each time recording the exact route, distance, fuel useage, whatever. Five circuits and each one recorded, timed, measured and pinned." The man seemed to shiver then, a short but violent tremor that almost blurred the edges of him and then he was still again and *Fuck*, thought Mallory, *where did that drink come from?* Because the man's glass was full again and Mallory could've sworn that he'd emptied it.

"And then we turned on the fuzzy logic circuits. I drove the first two laps and they were normal. I kept to the same lines and the car's travel data was the same." There was pride in the man's voice, the pride of a craftsman admiring his own work and not allowing false modesty to interfere with his pleasure of it. "I was in my element really, just driving and keeping everything the same, following the lines and speed signatures we'd agreed on.

"I like cars because of my dad," the man said, catching Mallory by surprise. "He never saw a speed limit he didn't want to break, and he could fix cars, enjoyed fixing them. Enjoying going fast was a way of being with Dad, you know?"

"Yes," said Mallory, because he did, thinking of his fraught relationship with his own father and how the only thing they could talk about without arguing was their memories of holidays and days out when Mallory was young.

"There was a bridge over a river near us and Dad used to accelerate as he approached it, especially if it was late at night, and we'd roar over it and on the other side we'd leave the road, just for a moment, and then drop, and my stomach used to feel like it was rising into my throat and it made me laugh and laugh. Well, on the third lap of the track there was a feeling like that. It hit me hard, just for a second, as though the car had suddenly lifted and dropped. The instrument panel seemed to shimmer and then everything was back to normal and I finished driving and then the car went to testing and everything was normal.

"Only it wasn't. I'd followed the exact line, the mapping systems we had in the car showed us that, but the odometer showed that the car had only travelled about ninety percent of the mile it was supposed to have covered, and the clock was just over thirty seconds behind all the other watches and clocks we checked it against. 'Fuzzy logic,' said Lorenz and he sounded so smug. Janey didn't reply, simply waited for the various data sets to download and you could see her gearing up to flatten his theory when the wheel information came though, looking forward to being proved right. Don't ever let anyone tell you scientists aren't competitive, by the way, because they are. They're like monkeys arguing over bananas.

"Anyway, data finally emerges on Janey's screen and we all saw her read it and her eyes went wide and she said loudly, 'No fucking way'. Every data set said the same thing, that the car had only travelled nine tenths of a mile, not a full mile. Every wheel agreed, the fuel consumption gauge agreed, the odometer agreed. Everyone had seen the car drive a mile, I'd *driven* the car a mile, but it had only travelled fifteen hundred and seventy three yards. 'Fuzzy logic,' said Lorenz. 'The universe's *maybe*.'

"'Again,' said Janey so I drove another circuit, then another. I ended doing another seventeen circuits that day and on six of them I felt that off, swirling sensation and each time I did the car had travelled less than a mile and the clock was a little behind everyone else's."

"That's amazing," said Mallory, not really believing the man. He checked his phone again but there was nothing from Marie. His own stomach was swirling now, knotting in tension. The man, apparently not picking up on Mallory's discomfort, said, "It was. Amazing, I mean. There was no way to predict when the Wobbles would happen – we started calling them the Wobbles after I told the team how it felt to drive through one of them – but they happened regularly, and each time the car would tell us that it had travelled between ten and twenty percent less that I had driven it."

The man suddenly jerked his head up and down violently, not once but several times, a nodding dog motion done at incredible speed. *That's got to hurt his neck*, thought Mallory, wondering if he'd got some kind of condition, a palsy or something similar, but the man didn't seem to notice. At the end of the motion he swallowed another drink, still showing no apparent ill-effects from the alcohol and how many had he had now? Mallory reached out for his own drink and stopped, startled as the man's hand shot out like a snake, took Mallory's glass and lifted it to his mouth, draining it and placing it back at the same speed. Again, the direction of the man's gaze didn't change and he made no indication that he realised what he'd done. Or maybe he simply didn't care. *Time to go*, thought Mallory and made to rise from his stool. His phone buzzed and he saw a message from Marie, *I'm waiting for you, you coming xx*

"I have to go," said Mallory. The man's hand, snakelike, shot out again and grabbed Mallory's wrist, grabbed it tight.

"Don't, not yet. Please, I need to tell someone. Just another minute." George, seeing the wrist grab, had stood, ever attuned the potential for trouble but Mallory nodded him away. The man's hand released him and then his arm was gone.

Not moved away but *gone*, back by his side without apparently passing across the space in-between.

"We tested it time and again. We attached trackers to other bits of the car, to me, and we drove it around the track and then on the roads around the testing centre, in all weathers and speeds. There was no pattern to the Wobbles but they ended up occurring in about fifteen percent of the journeys, and each time they did the car travelled around ten percent less than the track's length. Even Janey had to admit there was something going on, something potentially very special, even if she couldn't explain it. Lorenz, he was just about as smug as a man can get.

"I had my first Wobble eight days after the that initial one in the car. I was at home, walking from the kitchen to the bathroom when suddenly I was in the bathroom with no memory of the intervening steps and with my stomach churning like I'd swallowed something acidic."

"I thought you... wobbled?... in the car?" asked Mallory despite himself.

"I did. I mean, I wobbled for the first time not in the car. I wobbled without wanting to. I wobbled because the fucking fuzzy logic had jumped from the car to me because I was the only one who'd been in the car when it wobbled." For the first time the man's composure seemed to crack and he swallowed, loud and heavy, and then opened his mouth as though to scream. He jaws seemed to lock as though he was straining against it, against whatever was bubbling up his throat from his belly and sweat sprang out on his forehead and he made a noise like a stovetop kettle coming to the boil.

And then his mouth was closed and the sweat was gone from his forehead and he was silent.

Mallory took a step back. The air around the two seemed charged all of a sudden, heavy as though a storm was brewing around them. "I have to go," he said again as his phone buzzed, but he couldn't look at it because the man was turning to face him and his eyes were like holes torn in the fabric of his face to reveal something swirling and lost underneath, something desperate and unmoored and flailing.

"It's infected me," he said quietly. "There's no reason I can see, but that makes sense doesn't it? Fuzzy sense. Fuzzy *logic*, it's jumped from the car to me because I was in the car and now I wobble all the time and it's getting more frequent and I can't stop it."

Mallory took another step back. He didn't know what to say so said nothing as the man's head did that frantic, violent jerking again.

"I'm lost even when I'm here," said the man, "and I starting to lose where 'here' is. I start towards something and then I'm there or here or I'm somewhere else."

"I'm sorry, I really have to leave," said Mallory. "Thanks for the drink but my wife, she's expecting me." His phone buzzed and again this time he looked at it. Marie again, another single ? and that sense of a gathering storm was suddenly even thicker and he could almost see electricity and clouds and dust and he had to go, had to *be gone* and he turned and left as the man said again, "I'm lost.

"Please, help. I'm —"

His voice broke off partway through whatever he was saying. Walking out of the door, Mallory glanced back over his shoulder and saw that the bar was empty. The man was gone. Mallory wasn't surprised; already the meeting with him had taken on the sense of a fever dream and he was almost running now, needing to escape back to home, and even if he and Marie carried on arguing that was normal, that was reality, and he wanted that more than anything now.

The air had bruised to purple while he was in the bar, clouds gathering above him, and the air felt heavy and rich, dense with a terrible heft and weight and tautness, a balloon expanded to its utmost and about to burst and Mallory was moving fast through it, having to push against it, push forwards, and then one of the streetlamps flickered ahead of him and a shadow moved and his stomach hollowed and dropped and rose and he tasted bile.

There was a man in the street ahead of him, and Mallory was sure he hadn't been there a moment ago.

i

And it came to pass one winter's day, when the snow lay thick on the ground like a blanket of dead wishes, that a child was born. It was forced out from between its mother's heaving thighs and palpitating muscles in a wet slosh, a cork from a champagne bottle where only the stopper is important and not the vintage of the liquid that follows. In that pushed moment, new life came into the world. Slapped and shocked into breathing, the air cold and rough on its skin, the child began to pule and scream. Away and above, in the mountains to the West, a lonely and frost-ridden wolf howled a mournful note, and on the greying hearth in the ragged dwelling, the black pot whistled in off-key accompaniment.

The midwife, wrists and hands covered in the slick juices of that laborious birth, smiled just once, quickly and humourlessly. She stared down at the mother who lay sheened in sweat, legs wide and birthing slit open for the world to see. Ugly. The tiny mewling ball of blood and shit and snot in her hands wriggled strengthlessly, its eyes closed and its fingers and toes curling ferociously. Ugly. Above the midwife, the child and the empty mother, the skies stretched dark and black as solitude. She began the job of cleaning child and vessel, sighing gently.

It was cold in the land and Abraham, son of no one (for his father's name, like his mother's life and his own youth, was lost in the shadowed past), shivered. The fire that had heated his heart and belly for many years was dying, and he with it. He dribbled and lisped now, his limbs and head twitching whenever they fancied. When he walked, he listed to one side like a holed ship or a tree in a gale and only the strongest of efforts kept him from pitching over sideways when the more powerful of the elastic jerks hit him. It caused the villagers to avoid him, insult him, fling rocks at him but at least this gave him space and time and peace. Solitude had proved a surprisingly gentle mistress, giving him rest from the tumult of his earlier years. Gone, he reflected thankfully, were the days when there were people at his feet, often to kiss them but sometimes to pull them out from under him.

Left to himself in his hut of mud and shit, self-made and as tilted and turned as he himself was, Abraham studied the stars, the flights of birds and snowflakes and the guts of pigs. These things wrote his life and everyone else's life as accurately as an arrow wrote its way into a target and he had learned to read their text as surely as if it were engraved in stone. Their truth was proved time and time again, and they stood firm against all critics. And now they told him that the King was born, come to this earth at last; in a nearby valley and with the scent of poverty in his nostrils, the King had come. But the guts and the stars and the flight of hawks had also told Abraham that the winter was to get colder yet, and that the wind would blow over the land like the very breath of God. They told him that the King was come and yet was unrecognised in his birth. They told him that the King was in danger.

It took Abraham all of his strength, but he dragged himself into his thickest animal furs and ignoring his treacherous body's twitchings and flailings, went out to walk the hills. Through the cold and the dark, he went to pay fealty.

The child lay on its back in the crudely made crib and wondered. It was wrapped in wolf fur that prickled against his skin and was rough, although it was at least warm. Behind its closed eyelids, its blue eyes stared. It felt that all it had to do was to concentrate and it could look further, look through the thin skin to see the ceiling of the dwelling. Cracked and splintered, it would be able to see stars through it and clouds lowering and roiling across the sky like angry scorpions. It did not make the effort to do so yet, but instead, turned its attention upon itself.

He was male, he decided, because he was unlike the old woman who had dragged him into this place or the old whore who lay, arms and legs akimbo, on the bedding in the corner. He realised further things; that he was not loved by these two, nor did he have it in him to love them. That he was helpless as a child, and yet not a true child. He was... special. He could reason, plan, think thoughts that were more adult and complex than the whale-thighed piece of meat in the corner would be able to.

There was another in the hut as well as the two women and himself; a man, a slack-jawed, idiotic alcoholic who even now was shooting his seed into the woman who had acted as midwife at his only child's birth. This man thought himself father to the new child, but he was not, could not be. No, his real Father was above him, out past the hole-filled roof, past the clouds, past the stars, past even the sky itself.

His real Father had put him here for a reason, but of this knowledge he was dumb. It was a secret, hidden from him. The more he probed it, trying to discover what his real Father meant by placing him here, the more the reason slipped away from him, aching in its absence like a rotten tooth. Somewhere deep in his newly formed mind, a blood apple of hatred grew. He was helpless and yet his Father had deserted him here, with this grey meat mother asleep in the corner and his false father, still fucking in the cot. There were no reasons forthcoming, no touch of love or consolation for the child as he lay, hating, in his crib. It was a low, dirty slug of a trick. It was an action that deserved hatred, for their treatment of him was hateful. But also, through the anger, he began to feel another emotion.

He hurt, and he did not think that the hurting would stop for a long time.

Far beyond, in the Walled City, the tall man sat with his chin resting upon one hand. His eyes roamed across the marbled floor of his throne room, taking in arabesques and frescoes that showed great scenes from mythology and history. Flames leapt bright and warm in several fireplaces, keeping the cold and drear at bay. He was surrounded by beauty and imbued with power, yet the tall man was uneasy. His astrologers and soothsayers had seen the coming of a child who was to be King, but King of what, no one knew.

They (useless, scurrying cowards all) had further told the tall man that an idiot would be the only one who ever knelt to this new King, but that most everyone would pray to him. Both King and God! There lay power indeed! And yet, if this idiot was the only one to kneel, then was this King not simply a King of Idiots? And why should everyone pray to the King of Idiots? Such thoughts made the tall man's head ache sullenly. Being King of the Walled City was difficult enough without having to ferret meaning out of the signs read by his eager-to-please skywatchers. He shut his eyes and tried to think.

V

Abraham's progress, twitching and jittering over snow-encrusted hills and down ice-rimed valleys, was slow. The wind wrapped itself around him and pulled at his legs, trying to unbalance him, blistering his exposed skin and freezing the hair on his head. Falling snow reduced his vision to mere body lengths, and the night seemed ranged against him like some terrible, cold demon. The ground, when he fell against it, felt as hard as stone and the air itself cracked in the subzero temperatures. He was glad for his animal skins; they may have looked more natural on their owner wolves, but at least they kept out most of the cold. Some of the cold, anyway.

His spittle, which drooled continuously from the corner of his twisted mouth, had frozen into a small icicle encasing his skin and unwashed beard in its cold finger. His feet, wrapped in strips of leather and cloth, had passed through numbness and had started to burn with cold. In the distance, a wolf pack howled its presence, and each howl brought the pack closer. He did not have much time.

Trying to increase his speed, Abraham the cripple and idiot moved on, frantic.

The child heard his false father (oh, untrue creator!) and the midwife rise up from the cot after several hours of near-silence, a lack of noise broken only by the susurrations of breath from the three sleeping adults in the hut. The midwife and the man were talking, and although he could not discern specific meaning from the sounds, he still knew what they were saying. They were talking about him; him and his mother. He had apparently come early and caused her some trouble, which was why she now slept like a gutted hog in the corner. He wanted to smile at this knowledge, but found that controlling his muscles to do so was beyond him. He could breathe, he could feel his heart beating, but he could not exert authority over his body in any way. His fingers curled and straightened without being told to, his eyes stayed clenched shut even though he had tried to open them. More indignity that he would revenge later.

He was trying to decide upon a name for himself. He knew instinctively that he would have no influence over his naming in his earlier years, but that he could later drop whatever legend they gave him in favour of his own chosen title. He had a title, he knew, and although he did not know yet why, he had been sent to this benighted hovel. He understood, he hoped, that his specialness invested him with a power far above that of the people he felt sure he would meet, people like the three that were about him now. His title would be a title of some notice and power, to be respected. To be obeyed.

The two were still talking about him. His false father did not want him. Neither father, it seemed, wanted him. One (unbeknownst to the other) had placed him down here, the other thought he was... what? An inconvenience. An inconvenience to be dealt with... how? He could not understand exactly. Whatever it was, they were to do it before his slattern mother awoke. He heard the two come towards him and he could sense with horror the pair's intense, almost sexual, excitement. He managed to open his eyes a crack, focussed with difficulty and saw the woman's face, saw his false father's grimy, stubbled mask. He was lifted and carried aloft.

One last hill, and the wolves close at his heels. Abraham put his tiredness away and collapsed onwards, feeling as though he had somehow come adrift in the world. Everything was blank and white now, shrouded and shaded with incredible agony.

The crest of the hill. And then, to look down at last on the dwelling of the King.

And to see what they were doing.

Cold. He was cold. A feeling against him that was new, a pressure that was equal all over like the gentle caress of an all-encompassing hand.

They told him that the King was not to be a King of borders, but a King of minds. This, the tall man thought, was infinitely more dangerous. He wanted to rouse his armies from their slumber, to send them forth to hunt this new King out and kill him, but his seers stopped him. They told him to cease his concern, for this new King was not and could never be a threat to the tall man or his kingdom.

So cold it burned, oh, what had those miserable hated things done to him, and why didn't his real Father help? The gentle pressure was still there, but joined now by a new pressure inside. His chest felt wrong, inflated and burning and empty and full at the same time. There was something missing.

Air. He had no air. Where was his air?

The water trough.

They had him in the water, under layers of broken ice, in the water trough. He could see the child flailing pinkly, held down by the man and the woman. Abraham's shuddering body gave a huge twitch then, pitching him sideways. In shock, he tried to run, but could gain no speed. Choking on a great and terrible feeling of loss, he gave up the unequal struggle with his body. He could not run. He could not reach the child. Abraham fell to his knees and prayed.

Not so cold now. There was a flaming heat in his lungs, spreading and warming him from the inside out. And then there was a noise, heard over and under the pounding of the blood in his ears. A voice, saying of his welcome return, greeting him as a Father to his Son. Telling him he must have existed to be prayed to and called upon. Telling him that he had to have lived to die and be born again as a God.

You, said the voice, *have the prayers of all mothers- and fathers-to-be that will ever come. You will take their pleas and their desperate, quiet exhortations and their screamed invocations and proffered bargains and you will decide. You,* it said, *will have power beyond measure. You are the King of Unborn Children.*

Somewhere in the hut, the hog-stuck bitch opened her mouth and cried for her child and a first prayer went unanswered.

The Cave in the Mountain

I

How many sites did the Order have now, Lancaster wondered? It was something he'd never counted despite how assiduous he was about keeping the records up to date as the information came in, changing the colour of the ribbons around the pins dotting the map on the wall and writing the newly called into the heavy leather ledger in solid black ink, but actually counted? No. He sighed, rubbed his eyes and looked again at the map. So many pins, and still so many with yellow ribbons trailing from them; yellow for flame, yellow for light.

Yellow for safety.

Whatever their actual number, however safe the world still was because of the Order, there were definitely fewer yellows these days. He had tried to avoid this truth but it was becoming inescapable. The Order had fewer capable, active called on its roster and more and more older, weaker members. More and more gaps.

Grey ribbons for where the Order had managed to arrange temporary cover or where the dweller was alone and old, black for where there was no-one to maintain the light. Recently, there were more blacks, too many; too many blacks and a growing number of grey.

Time was the Order had spare called, could fill any gap that occurred with ease, could cover the times that people were ill or needed a rest and time to find themselves again. Someone would be sent. Hell, Lancaster thought, smiling, most of the sites had more than one resident and they could fill in for each other rather than need to call on outside resources. Lancaster himself had run away, twice, after his calling and both times his space in the barrier against the darkness had been filled by his teacher, and latterly his friend, Ash and the others who used to live in the cave, all of them a little community bound by light and dark. The first time he ran he had tried to go home and that had hurt because 'home' no longer remembered him, and the second he had just run and run and run until he realised that there was nowhere to run to, and then he had gone back and never left again. He no longer remembered what home had been. The world would scab around his absence, he had been told by Ash, but Ash had never told him that his own memories of what had been his world would scab over within him so that there was just this existence for him, this and nothing else.

Black ribbons, and grey, and fewer yellow. *We're dying*, he thought, *the Order is dying.*

There was a guttering noise behind him and the light in the room wavered, sputtered, flared and then faded. It didn't extinguish, though, merely dimmed slightly. Lancaster looked over at the crack in the wall and saw that one of the candles set in the sconces at four points around it had burned out. The other three were still burning, had different amounts of time left in them, deliberately set to never finish at the same moment. Lancaster glanced at his watch. The candle had burned out earlier than he had expected and now that he looked, the others were lower than they should be. Had they changed suppliers? Started using cheaper, inferior candles? He made a note to check, scrawling it on a sticky label and gumming it to the front of the ledger where he was bound to see it, and then took a new candle from the pile in the alcove and went to the crack.

The darkness was already escaping.

It was slow, held back by the other candles' light, but still it came, unspooling from the edge of the ragged tear in the rock like a black snake, slithering down and spreading as it went. It flowed around the lumps and crevasses in the uneven wall, covering the rock face so that soon only the tips of the ridges were visible within it like atolls rising from a dark and terrible sea glimpsed from above.

Every time he watched it, Lancaster became fascinated with it again. There was something dangerously hypnotic about it, something dangerously *seductive*. It was easy to imagine simply watching this flowing tide, not moving against it, not challenging it, just watching and loving it and seeing in its depths every promise ever made, every gift ever given, until it rose high enough to swallow the world and left nothing but itself behind.

That's how it happens, he thought as he leaned and put the candle into the sconce, forcing it down onto the spike. Already the screwed-down feet of the sconce were lost to the inky, creeping dim. It wasn't full black yet, he saw, the rusted bolts of the sconce still just visible through it, but it wasn't far off, was thickening and darkening every moment.

Lancaster lit the candle.

The sudden flare of light from the match and the extra illumination once the wick caught drove the dark back, but not entirely. It still lapped just below the crack's edges, a wound that was old, older than almost everything, yet was still infected and raw. *It's getting defiant*, he thought and took a small, cheap LED torch from his pocket. The beam, bright even against the light of the candles, played over the dark's surface. It swayed, reared up against him and he thought again of a snake, threatened and threatening, and then it fell back and the crack was just a crack again. Lancaster turned off the torch, waited to make sure the darkness wasn't feinting, didn't come flowing back, but all was still. It was gone, for now.

II

The Order did use computers and emails and cell phones but the problem was that the darkness like to creep in the world in out of the way spots where it wouldn't be noticed until it was too late, on islands in bays where people rarely went or the lowest points of deep ravines or caves, and technology rarely worked well in these places. Besides, Lancaster thought, the Order almost certainly preferred things the way they were, the way they had always been. Oil lanterns and candles seemed to hold the darkness back better than electric lights or any bank of lamps anyway, and writing in pen in heavy ledgers seemed to have a permanence that databases and lines in emails did not. The ledger Lancaster was using currently had entries that dated back almost a century, the others on the shelves could track the Order back a thousand years or more, and somewhere he liked to imagine there might be marks on rocks made before the Order was the Order and before John of Patmos saw the darkness leak out and trace its fingers across his face in four greasy lines, marks that spoke of prehistoric man's attempts to use burning mammoth fat to fill the air with fetid, life-affirming light to keep the dark at bay. It meant that Lancaster got most of his communications and updates by letter, often handwritten, always days or weeks after they had been penned. Today there were three, and he recorded their contents faithfully.

The old priest that had lived in the church on the island in the bay in the Aegean had finally succumbed to his cancer but that was okay. He had served long, and well, and there was a girl who had been called to him several years ago who would now fulfil the duties needed and would continue the work.

The hole the Order had discovered in the basement of the building in the small city in South America was gone, effectively blocked when the building's foundations were strengthened and new concrete poured. The Order would need to keep monitoring the site, of course, and the building and its occupants would still be susceptible to illnesses and malaises and glowering, black moods, but there would be no need to leave a permanent station there. That was good as it freed up the site's called to be, pun definitely intended, called upon to serve at a new station.

The third was the most worrying. High in the hills above Kobu Prefecture the called who tended to a shrine, ostensibly to Shinto gods but which was in actuality to keep the light burning to trap what was under the building, was ill. Not dead, thank the Light, not even incapacitated, but ill nonetheless and growing iller, his insides decaying, and no new called had appeared to take the mantle from him.

Lancaster had a theory. Some in the Order thought that fewer were called because the darkness was finally winning, was corrupting people away from the light and that the call itself was lost, but not Lancaster. He thought that the call itself was corrupted, not because of darkness but because of *noise*. The world was just too busy, too noisy, and the call, when it came, was not lost but simply misheard, distorted, buried under the weight of all the other things that people heard every moment of every day. It explained so much, he thought, because the world *needed* explaining. How else could you understand what people did, the things they fixated upon, unless you accepted that they were hearing a call but hearing it wrong? People were being drawn not to the light but to the *lighted*, things light in their way but not the light itself, not the light that held back the dark. They heard the call and became focussed on the screen that fed them information or the pill that they were told would slim them or cleanse their insides, on the device that allowed them to communicate with people a world away or that allowed them to watch people rutting with each other or killing each other, and they sought meaning in these things because the call was out of tune, was buckled into something warped and wrong under the mass of other calls and other noises.

The Order wasn't being beaten, wasn't struggling, it was fucking drowning.

A few years ago, in an attempt to modernise, or at least organise, the Order's resources, Lancaster had sent out questionnaires for any new or recently called to fill in. From his base in the cave he hoped to pull together a list of the skills and talents and interests the called possessed, hoping that although the world had forgotten them and they the world they came from, people would still retain the things they had learned and some of the experiences they had put this learning towards. He had some vague notion that the Order might be able to move the called around from site to site, partly to stop them becoming bored or complacent but mostly because it made sense, didn't it? To send a called with computer skills to one of the few sites where there was web access and where the IT worked, to send another with skills in geology to a site where the natural terrain might be used to block a gap or in some other way hinder the darkness, that was surely sensible?

It had come to nothing. Most of the called filled in the questionnaires, yes, but any suggestions Lancaster had made for reassignment of the called to new sites had been resisted by the Order itself. The called, he was summarily informed, were summoned to a specific place at a specific time and to move them except in the most unusual of circumstances risked them losing the call. Lancaster still had the paperwork, yellowing and wrinkling, in a file in one of the rooms here. Sometimes he thought about burning it, but didn't because deep inside himself was a nagging desire to somehow make it work, for the Order to embrace the possibilities that change and mobility could offer. Until then, he waited.

Later, he updated the map. He changed one ribbon from yellow to grey and another to white to show that the dark had, at that site at least, been driven back. Lancaster tried to count the pins but they were so jumbled, clustered heavily in some places and sparsely in others with no apparent pattern that he kept losing track and eventually gave up. It didn't help that the map itself was old and covered in drawn and redrawn lines as countries' borders changed. The places of darkness never changed, of course, but the government in charge of the areas often did. One year the Order would need to watch this government's attitude to the site, the next year another's, and accommodations and arrangements made, bribes paid, contracts negotiated. He wondered if that's what had happened with the candles, a new set of political masters taking over leading to a new set of supply and demand chain deals being done and undone.

Did anyone know the total tally of places called to and called inhabiting them? Was anyone but him even keeping records, he wondered, and then wondered about his wondering. *I've no one to talk to but myself,* he thought, *and I've heard everything I've got to say a thousand times before.* All his concerns and fears, all his moans and groans, all his ideas and arguments, they rattled in him like marbles in a tin, clattering and aimless and known. What did it matter if he knew how many sites there were? Would it help the Order to quantify the amount of darkness seeping into the world? Would it help to know about each called and what they knew? No. It was a symptom of his need for order, of his need for control, nothing more. Some of the called forgot more than he, he knew, losing not just their specific lives but their countries, their religions, their everything, so focussed were they in their call and the light and the dark. Not him, though; he fought to keep as much as he could, not knowing which of it might prove useful one day. He gathered information around him like a cloak. It was why, he supposed, he'd ended up as record-keeper, because even the Order sometimes recognised a skill and utilised it. Somewhere, there must be accountants and managers and assistants, all working to keep the Order afloat.

Were there planners? Strategists? Lancaster didn't think so. That implied action not mere reaction, and the Order was not active in the truest sense of the word. It waited, and it only moved when the holes revealed themselves because that's what John, the sainted, beloved, addled John of Patmos, had done. He had wandered, stumbled across an old well and recognised the darkness crawling up from within it, and it had broken him, twisting him into a raving paranoid whose head was filled with images of horsemen and trumpets and the end of the world but who knew the power of the light. The Order walked in his shadow, and it followed his steps.

Lancaster couldn't remember, was 'Lancaster' his first name or his last? Or a name he'd simply adopted?

He reread the entry in the journal, the second most recent one, about the hole being blocked by the building work. Had anyone asked why? More importantly, had they asked if the same tactic could be used at other sites? Could they block holes and the darkness with concrete, or rock falls, or plugs of masonry? "Has anyone ever asked," he said aloud, turning to face the crack in the wall, "can we just tell the sainted John's horsemen to simply fuck off?"

III

Lancaster was, he knew, lucky. Some of the called lived lives that couldn't, with the best will in the world, even be called spartan. His own site was in a cave that had been expanded and made habitable by troops in the second global conflict, although troops of which side Lancaster had never been able to find out. It had been a munitions cache, and with the munitions gone the space had been made relatively comfortable. It was dry and held to a constant temperature, had sleeping areas with beds, and there were separate storage areas. He had a generator and, away from the crack and its guard of candle-bearing sconces, strings of light dangled from electric cables tethered to the ceilings. It was protected from the worst of the winter snows and summer storms equally. It was home.

Others in the Order lived in shacks, in tents or wood huts, without electricity or water, without any light other than that which they kept around the hole or pit or crack they were guarding, and it made no sense. Surely the Order could build them a home that contained some comforts, some softness to hold them when the night felt endless and their old lives weighed as heavy as a suffocating blanket and the faces of people they had forgotten and who had forgotten them hung above them and spoke to them, silent and voiceless and louder than any other sound across the world? It was as though the Order wanted them to be hermits, to enforce an ascetic lifestyle upon them, to force them to remain at the rockface, digging away at the darkness and never having space to stop and wonder if things could or should be better. *Perhaps it's fear,* he thought, *fear that if they let us have some comfort we'll want more, want it all back, and that we'd run in search of it,* and in his head a small voice said, *And perhaps they're right.*

Lancaster changed another candle and then, later, another, and each time he looked into the dark to see if he could discern any kind of sense to what he was doing but saw only shadows.

The next morning, he replaced another candle and updated the records. For once, a new called had found their way to a site and the Order could be reassured, for a while, that it could win. Lancaster wrote it all, and kept the light burning.

IV

How many years had he been here? At first, he had kept a clear track but soon it became easier not to bother. He knew the date, of course, and could probably work out his length of tenure if he tried, but keeping track felt like it contained the assumption of an end point and, of course, there wasn't. There was no beginning to this, no end, only the light and the dark.

Another candle.

Another.

Another.

Another, and Lancaster slept and woke and lit another candle. He must have eaten and he must have shit and he must have washed and he must have drunk, but he remembered none of it. His whole life had collapsed down to just two elements, the light and the dark, the dark and the light.

The candle and the crack.

In his cave in the hills Lancaster put his head in his hands and wept.

V

He carried on, because what else was there to do? The light was still needed and the dark still promised, and one still had to face the other. In between updating the records (another called, another death, a new site discovered in a cellar in a tiny town in the north of England), Lancaster wrote another letter to the Order's head. He didn't know their name, or names, whether there was one person or more or if there even was a 'head', but he wrote anyway. The letters went to a central point, all their communications did, and were sent on so he had no idea where any kind of head or council might be based. Patmos, he had always assumed, but it could just as easily have been Antarctica or a suburb in notown USA or grimtown England or just past the range of hills in which the cave he called home was situated.

It could be anywhere.

In the letter, Lancaster urged the Order to do more than just react. Plan, he said, experiment. Can we block the holes? Can we go out and recruit rather than simply wait for people to hear the calling? Can we use hired staff, give some of the called a break or cover when they were ill? In the letter, Lancaster urged the Order to modernise.

The reply, when it came, was handwritten on paper that was thick and which had yellowed in the sun, the Order's symbol at the head of the page faded to almost nothing. The paper felt old, and the message it contained older: *We thank you for your comments, record keeper, but for now we carry on as ever, the balance between the light and the dark, the fulcrum on which the balance of the world rests. Perhaps we might look at these suggestions in the future.*

Perhaps we may grant your suggestions air to breathe just as we start to suffocate.

Or drown.

Lancaster crumpled the reply and threw it to the cave's floor, then picked it up and smoothed it out. He punched holes in its left margin and placed it in the file with all the others, another record kept safe for future generations to read and marvel at.

Another candle.

Another.

Another fucking candle.

He took to sitting watching as the candles guttered out, keeping the dark at bay with his torch, the lance-bright beam tearing at the edges of the black, flowing stream like a finger picking at wet paper, leaving shreds across the rock face. Lancaster played with the dark, letting it creep as far as his feet before driving it back, letting it have the hope of escape before pinning it, corralling it, forcing it away.

Before lighting another candle.

Sometimes, he spoke to it. He told it of the things he'd lost, the things he remembered, and of them which he missed the most. Oddly, these were things and events rather than people; he missed fresh pizza, he missed opening presents on his birthday, he missed long lie-ins, he missed midnight church services on Christmas Eve, he missed the last day of work before holidays and the feeling of having time to use just as he saw fit, he missed conversations about movies and music and books.

He missed movies and music and books.

Lancaster told the dark about the hopes he'd had and the dreams he still had, and knew that some of them weren't even real, were things he'd created since he'd arrived here to try to fill and explain the growing space inside him. He told the dark his fears. He told the dark his desires. He told the dark everything, and then he told it again for what else was there?

The dark did not reply.

Another candle.

Another, and ah *Jesus* would this never end? Was this it, and endless replay of lighting wick after wick, the grease of candlewax always under his nails, the smell of burning always in his nostrils, his clothes slowly decaying and the Order replacing them each time with cheap shirts and trousers, cheaper shoes, the same things sent to every called until they all looked alike, an interchangeable army of nameless, faceless people growing older in anonymous, lonesome nowheres? Was this Hell? Had he died and gone to Hell, and no one had told him?

Another candle.

Lancaster had no alcohol, another rule by the Order, so the promise of temporary oblivion was denied him. Instead, he cried, and he raged, and he lit candles.

VI

"Perhaps there should be a handbook," Lancaster said out loud, speaking to the dark. A long trail of it had reached the floor and he played his torch beam in front of it, forcing it to slow and stay close to the wall, "all split into useful chapters. 'How to Cope if You're Alone'. 'Long Nights With Yourself'. 'Getting the Best from Your Cave'. 'Good Candle Care'. That kind of thing. What do you think?"

The dark did not reply. Two of the candles were out now and one of the remaining two was burning dangerously low. What would happen if it went out and the torch batteries failed, he wondered? Would a single candle hold it at bay while he lit new ones, or would it have the strength to move through the pale light and make its way out into the world?

And would it matter if it did, if he let it escape?

Best not to find out. Lancaster lit a candle, waited a while and then lit another and then, a further while later, yet another to replace the nearly dead one and the crack was again surrounded by the gleam and dance of flame and the dark shrank away and hid itself from his eyes.

That night, he forgot the candles.

He awoke more rested that he could remember being for a long time and for a few wonderful seconds he could think he was over the hump of whatever this mood was before realising the cheap alarm clock had stopped at 2.35a.m., twenty five minutes before the alarm was due to wake him to replace the next candle. What time was it now? Sunlight filled the entrance to the cave so morning, late fucking morning, hours after he should have attended to the crack. He fled his bed and ran, ran and cried out as he ran, calling the name of the person he used to be, remembering it and screaming it out as though to summon that person back into being. No one answered his cries.

The dark was out and over the floor, two candles extinguished and a third guttering, spattering light in uneven gobbets around the walls and he had no torch with him to drive it back and had to step in it to reach the sconces, grabbing candles from the pile as he ran past. The dark was spreading towards the pile of pale wax cylinders, he saw, as though to flow over them and somehow smother them, hide them from him. Could it think like that? Did it plan? Imagine?

Strategise?

Why had his alarm failed?

There was no time to think about it now. He high-kicked through the covering scum of black, trying to bounce off the floor and be in contact with it as little as possible because in the brief moments his feet were in the dark it was foul, its warmth as dry and tender as the hug of a loved one, a promise that vibrated up through his body more sensual or erotic than that of any lover, and how easy to stop, to let it happen, to lay down and let it cover him and for this to be over. So easy. So, so easy.

No. This was what he had been called for, and he would do it whether he liked it or not. A candle.

Another.

A third, this held in his hand and swept around, driving the already retreating shadows back to the crack heedless of the wax that dripped onto his hand in hot trickles and the memory of a voice that whispered to him to come, to come to it, to come back to the world and all the sensations that world contained and all the places those sensations could take him.

Finally, when it was contained, Lancaster let himself collapse to the floor and tried to catch his breath. As he peeled pennies of solidified wax off his hands he stared at the crack and imagined the dark staring back at him and smiling, waiting for its next opportunity, for his next mistake. His hands were covered in red marks and his lungs burned.

After, Lancaster went back to the desk on which the ledgers sat. He wrote an account of the incident into the ledger that recorded the history of his own site and then went to replace the batteries in his alarm clock. He set the time using his wristwatch, and then the alarm by judging when the next candle would need replacing. Finally, he wrote another letter to the head (or heads) of the Order setting out his mistake, his actions and his worries that the darkness had somehow recognised the threat the pile of unused candles posed to it and had tried to act against them. He also told them of his recent troubles and moods, sparing nothing, asked for help and put the letter with the correspondence to be taken with the next delivery and collection.

VII

The Order didn't require religious belief in the called, but it was religious – how could it not be, given its founder – so Lancaster imagined that the head or heads of the Order looked like members of the Greek Orthodox Church, all beards and piercing eyes and robes tied with thick braids of rope, the women in heavy dresses with lace headscarves. Both sexes, he thought, would keep their hair long, so in an act of childish rebellion he started to shave his head and beard every day. He had asked for clippers several years ago but been refused and supplied, instead, with a pair of heavy scissors, a straight razor and a strop, and he started to use this. At first he was a mass of nicks, his head and face and neck slicked with blood after each shave, but he soon became proficient at it, and his skin was smooth and unmarked. *I will not look like you,* he thought each time he let the razor fall through the soap and cleave stubble from skin, watching as suds and bristle fell into the basin in front of him. *I am still me, whoever me is.*

Whoever me is. He didn't recognise the face that looked back at him from the shaving mirror as the person he had been. How many photographs of himself had he seen, had existed, before he had been called? Hundreds? Thousands? It was impossible to exist out there without having your image caught, imprisoned, almost every day, but here there was just a cracked mirror in a room lit with pale bulbs and he didn't remember himself as he'd been. There was just this man ahead of him, whoever he was.

Lancaster's skin was pale from all his time in the cave. He thought his eyes might have been blue once but now they were a washed-out grey, loaded with shadows, webbed with their own darkness. Another sweep of the razor cleared another swathe of hair. He tried to smile at himself but it looked forced and empty and he stopped.

The letter had been taken yesterday. He could, he thought, expect a reply in a week or so, maybe a little more. He had hopes they might listen this time; after all, he had almost let it escape, had almost failed in his duties. Surely they would have to do something?

Another candle.

Another, the smell of wax so thick in his nose that he imagined he could dig it out with a fingernail, the smell of burning so strong in the cave that it was like a physical thing, a floating miasma coating his skin that that he never managed to fully clean off. He felt, some days, like he could reach out and grasp it, pull it down from the air like skeins of floating muslin.

Another.

Another.

Another, and again and again and again.

VIII

We thank you for your comments, record keeper, but for now....

IX

Lancaster gathered rocks from the ground outside the cave and put them into the crack, fitting them into it and then removing them, a puzzle in which the aim was to eliminate gaps as far as possible. The dark, pushed further and further back into the crevasse by the torches Lancaster had balanced on boxes around the opening and pointed into it, glowered at him but could not move forward. He needed to show them, because if they would not respond to failure then maybe they would respond to success.

A piece here, another there, the spaces between them as thin as spiderwebs, building up from the bottom and two or three layers thick. A piece out, turned, and placed back in so that its unseen point pushed further into the crack's throat, choking it, and its base jammed firm between the pieces either side to form a good seal. Lancaster built a wall.

Lancaster had scoured through his stores the previous night, moving the sacks of dry goods and cans of fruit and vegetables, searching. He had no plaster or concrete, he found, but he did have several thick tubes of epoxy that might work. There was also flour, and because he rarely made his own bread there were sacks of it, the older ones filled with some kind of tiny weevil that looked like perambulatory rice grains. That might also work, he thought, and experimented, mixing it with water and stirring and eventually coming up with a mix like a thick glue when wet but which dried to the consistency of stone.

Perfect.

When he had filled the crack as best he could, reducing the gaps in its face to little more than a network of shadowlines, he made some more of the flour mixture, fossilising the weevils in the process, and ladled it into the lines, filling them so that no space remained. Then, as it was drying but before it was solid, he covered the entire wall with a thick layer of epoxy, creating a face into which he jammed thick planks left over from the war, wedging them in place with packing cases filled with sacks of flour. When it was all dry he'd try to buttress the planks with other planks forced up against them at angles and fixed to the floor of the cave. He might not be able to put a building on top of the hole but he could create its equivalent. He could block the crack. He kept the candles lit as he worked, and while his plug dried.

Another candle.

Another.

Morning, and time to light another and Lancaster found a mess of rock and dust and wood at the base of the wall below the crack, the crack itself open and the darkness shimmering within. The dried epoxy caught the candlelight in dull streaks and looked like the remains of an eggshell, cracked and splintered as the thing inside it birthed.

Lancaster cleared away the mess and wrote it up. He kept the records and now, he realised, the records were keeping him, had always kept him as he replicated action after action, trapped in the amber of routine and duty, always balancing, always just *there*.

Another candle.
Another day.
Another week.

X

There was a natural pool several hundred yards above the cave's mouth, fed by streams and rainwater trickles. Its water was usually cold but now, in summer, it attained a cool pleasantness that Lancaster enjoyed. He could strip, float on its surface or dive into its depths, and be someone else. With his Order-sent clothes abandoned, wearing only his skin, he was anybody, was everybody.

Wasn't Lancaster.

After clearing up the mess of his failure, Lancaster went to the pool and let himself drift, emptying himself of everything. This was it, then; this was life. No attempt to block the dark he could try would work, and the Order had decided that the maintenance of balance was simply where things were now, no changes required. We thank you for your comments. So be it.

There was a bird on the rocks at the edge of the pool, rapidly dipping its head in and out of the water, sending spray behind itself, fluffing its feathers and grooming itself. It looked bedraggled, insignificant against the background of the mountain, its tiny eyes glittering with stupidity and repetition. *That's us*, thought Lancaster, *that's us all over, cleaning ourselves in the light as the pool of darkness plays against our feet. Why won't they fight? Why won't they try?* Lancaster had a sudden image of the elders of the Order, whoever they were, a group of men and women posed, some sitting and others standing, all dressed in robes and long headdresses, the men bearded, the women plain-faced. The image appeared to him as a daguerreotype, old, edges cracked and wrinkled, focus depth varying over the surface of the picture, figures staring at the camera while behind them, unseen, the darkness came.

It boiled towards them, slipping about their ankles as they posed and waited, curling up below the hems of robes and dresses, long tendrils of dry warm shadow curling around knees and thighs, slipping around genitalia, narrowing as it rose and forming long thin fingers that probed and inserted themselves into anuses and vaginas, coiling into bowels and uteruses and intestines and still they did not move, still they sat, still they did nothing.

And then their eyes filled with blackness, their mouths spilled it out, their nostrils flooded with it until they were just the darkness clothed and on it came, wearing them like a Sunday Best outfit, making them talk. "We thank you," they said and their voice was a single sound, seductive as a promise in the heart of the night, "we thank you, we thank you, we thank you," and Lancaster was crying again but it didn't matter because his tears were just water, water falling into more water, and who would notice the extra or care or record its presence?

Above him, the mountain was shadowed and below the darkness waited and the candles burned.

XI

He had them all, not inside but out by the entrance, piled together on a pyre of wood and paper. He lit a match, put the flame to the edge of a sheet, waited until it caught, moved around and lit another section, and then another. The flames licked up, fed themselves, licked higher.

Then, he watched.

A candle burned, melted, the wax pooling down, bubbling. The candle above it, drooping lower, embraced the flame and started to melt to nothing. Another candle burned. Another. Another, and then all the candles burned, bright for now, while below the darkness waited.

Lancaster set fire to forever.

Afterword

I started writing this Afterword drinking wine whilst looking out over the flat, blue Mediterranean that I'd just had a long swim in, following what might count as the busiest and most exhausting few of months of my professional life.

I say this not to garner any kind of sympathy, by the way. I know that drinking wine whilst looking out over a flat blue Mediterranean that I've just swum in puts me squarely into the "lucky bastard" category of people, no matter what the preceding months looked like and no matter what pressures they've heaped on me. No, I mention it because its drinking wine and looking out over a flat, blue Mediterranean that I've just swum in that's allowing me the space to think back over the development of this collection and the stories it contains.

If you've got this far and are still reading, I'm assuming you're like me and enjoy this part of things, the author rambling on about their process, the things that lead to the stories, the influences and ideas behind them. Good. Bear with me, I'll try to make it make sense and keep it interesting.

The run up to the Mediterranean swimming, perusal and wine imbibing was professionally frantic, with four deadlines for major tasks occurring within 8 days of each other, and I ended up as frazzled as I've ever been. I think I survived only because of the support and encouragement and understanding of my loved ones, the regular intake of unhealthy junk food, not enough sleep and the thought that each was one day closer to popping out on the other side of that period, a bubble bursting forth from some very sharp turbulent brew.

And somewhere in the middle of all this, because of promises made and a deadline looming, I remembered I had to put a collection together. My initial thought was to create something new for my on-again off-again central character/hero Richard Nakata to investigate, but the timing didn't feel right for that. Then I wondered if I could write some of the stories that Nakata had collected about the place he now lived, the doom-soaked, rumour-laden and possibly cursed town of Martledge, but that didn't quite feel right either[1]. Instead, I kept thinking about some of the stories I'd

---

1 For those interested in this, don't worry, both of these collections will happen. Nakata is anything but a spent force...

written but hadn't ever found suitable homes for, and began to realise that they fitted together surprisingly well. They aren't about the same things, but in a way they are: fragility and the faceless mechanisms that rule us, things going wrong in unexpected directions, bad turns and worse luck, and from this I had a vague way forward.

It started with the writing of a new story, punched out in two marathon sessions, continued with casting my eye over already-finalised edits of two others to make sure they were good and done, and ended with a long day of further revisions to three other homeless things, cutting and adding and reworking them so that they resembled stories I felt could be shown to people rather than hidden in a dusty folder in a hidden file on my MacBook. Finally, everything seemed to be as good as I could get it and I winged them off to Steve Shaw, editor and boss man of Black Shuck Books. I told Steve to be honest with me and he was, and between us we whipped *A Gathering of the Morose* into its final shape. So here it is, and I hope you've enjoyed it.

I'm not going to tell you about the story that Steve cut out. That's for another day and another book.

Coel Coeth

The only reprint in *A Gathering of the Morose*, this was originally written for an anthology of Halloween stories from which it was rejected for not being American enough. I always liked it, and it's not being American enough seemed a benefit rather than a problem to me so I kept an eye open with the vague idea that it might fit a more open anthology call. In the end, though, it was published as a bonus story in the paperback reprint of my PS Publishing collection, *Strange Gateways*[2], a fact I'd forgotten until Steve Shaw pointed it out to me. There's not an obvious influence behind this one, expect possibly the film *Ringu* and its doomed, tragic villain Sadako. I wanted, I think, to create something in which the terror crept rather than ran, but I also wanted to write a story in which the protagonist wasn't alone in seeing the world fall apart, even if the fact he has company doesn't actually help him at all...

When the Devil Took a Drink

This was written in the first Covid lockdown, the only thing I wrote in that curious, dreamlike three months in which I didn't wear long trousers

---

2   Still available kids, just go to the PS Publishing website!

or socks once and in which I watched an 80s movie a day. My wife, Rosie, was a community nurse at the time and went out each day into homes where people were dying from Covid and its complications, and there was something in the contrast between the sheer exhaustion and horror she was living with each day and my lazy, stay-at-home life that made me think of folk horror, the way the tone is often languid but the contents are nightmarish (read some Manly Wade Wellman, you'll see what I mean). I had wanted to revisit Martledge since writing *The Martledge Variations*[3] and add to its curses, and who better to curse it with than the Devil himself? This tale has been rewritten a couple of times, once to make it fit a story reading done on Halloween night in a nearby town and once to alarm the ladies of a local WI group, but the version presented here is the original and still my favourite. Manly Wade Wellman is a key influence on it, obviously, but so are those local books you find in every town detailing the local history of the supernatural and arcane. They're great reads, and I urge you to hunt them out – they're a fun way to learn about your local environment.

---

3   Also still available, only this time you'll have go to the Black Shuck Books website and all will be revealed!

<u>The Fools' Parade</u>

An old story that I could never let go of, 'The Fools' Parade' was originally written while I was at university and has been re-written, punched, battered and generally fucked around with on a number of occasions since. I've never submitted it anywhere because I never found anywhere that it felt like it would fit, but I always thought it *should* fit somewhere, and I'm glad it found its place here. I'm not scared of clowns, but I have always thought that comedians make for very fine villains and villains make very fine comedians, and the image of a trail of them descending from the hills to both entertain and then punish (if that's what they're doing, I've never been quite sure) was the first part of this tale to emerge in my head and its one I still see on occasion, when I'm tired or when the world seems dark, those grinning, juggling, dancing people approaching slowly to cast their judgement about the place like coins in a fountain. The influences for this story are mostly lost to time, but I do know that I was trying to channel the great Dave Hutchinson's early work when I first wrote it, particularly his story about a man who needed to keep his job. All of his work is great, by the way but his early collections[4] are brilliant and unsettling and were a huge early influence on me.

---

4 *The Paradise Equation, Fool's Gold, Thumbprints* and *Torn Air* – all are fairly easy to find, and I'd urge you to give them a go!

The Half-Lost Man

I'd been reading a lot of J G Ballard (and so should you, especially if you haven't already) and was enjoying the rather dry tone he used, especially in his shorter works. I'm not sure where 'The Half-Lost Man' itself came from, but I think it may have been one of those rare occasions where I had a title but no story to go with it – usually with me the title is the last thing I come up with – and my Ballard-inspired brain drew this together from the starting point of, Why would someone be half-lost? How did they get to be like that, and what would it look like if they did? I think there's a bit of King's 'Mrs Todd's Shortcut' in here as well, and probably some *Event Horizon*. It's one of two new short stories written in 2025, which is slow for me compared to how much I wrote when I was first getting published, but more than I've managed for the previous couple of years because of life stuff, and I like it a lot. O'Dowd's seems like a nice place to drink, and I may go back there one day to see who else has popped in.

...And a King is Come

Another one from around the time of 'The Fools' Parade', another that's been beaten and battered but has always come out unbowed. Its had a number of different titles – my own preferred title has always been the first, 'The

King of Unborn Children', but a number of people told me that it gave the ending away, which I grudgingly accept is true. It's an oddly angry story from a time when I wasn't particularly angry, so much so that in editing it for this collection I had to tone it back a little. The younger me, and I suppose the interim me as well given I've revisited the story on a number of occasions since its first emergence, was a little too liberal with unpleasant ways to describe women which sort of fits this narrative (all the people in this story bar one are fairly horrible I think) but I also saw that I sort of went too far. I think I found a decent middle ground. A key influence for this story is Nick Cave, especially his astonishing novel *And the Ass Saw The Angel*, which I saw him do a reading from not long before writing the original version of this. There's something biblical in Cave's work, and I was definitely trying to ride his coattails here.

The Cave in the Mountain

Long-time readers (are you there? do you exist?) may remember that my first published story was called 'The Church on the Island', which was published in an Ash Tree Press anthology (*At Ease with the Dead*) and then republished in volume 19 of *The Mammoth Book of Best New Horror*, edited by the incomparable Steve Jones. It's the story that put me on the map, no matter how little my pin is, and I'll always love it, especially as it got me a World Fantasy Award nomination.

I'd always wondered what happened after the story finished, and in 2019 I got the chance to find out when, completely by chance, my wife Rosie booked us a last-minute break that turned out to be in the same resort that I'd written the first story in about 8 years earlier. On the first morning there, sitting at the bar table and looking out to that little blue church on the tiny island in the bay (there's a theme developing isn't there? Wine, the Mediterranean, sitting staring out aimlessly on holiday...) I suddenly realised what happened next wasn't about Charlotte or an old, weary priest but about someone else in the Order. By the time I returned home, a week later, the story was written just as the first had been, in longhand in a notebook whilst sitting at a table in the sun drinking coffee and marvelling at the turns and twists that had brought my life to this point. Divorce, remarriage, children, work and family shit all looping around and around until I found myself happier than I'd ever been, relaxed and in love and loved, sitting in the sun swimming in a pool knowing there's food and wine in my near future, writing about the end of the world. It does not, I think, get any better than that.

A note: The title of this Shadows collection, *A Gathering of the Morose* comes from one of Spike Milligan's war memoirs, I think probably *Where*

Have All The Bullets Gone? If you have any interest in WWII or military history generally, I'd urge you to read them – they're of their time, so sometimes racist, sometimes sexist – but they're beautifully written, hysterically funny and sometimes very sad, often on the same page. They're lyrical and true and give what I suspect is one of the few properly honest accounts of being a drafted soldier in the UK in that terrible, awful war. Spike died on February 27th 2002 and there isn't a week that passes without me thinking of something he wrote or said or did that made me laugh, and occasionally cry. Go and listen to *The Goon Show*, go and read *Puckoon* or his war memoirs, because trust me, you won't regret it. You can thank me later.

~

No book is written alone, even small ones like this – although it's me that does most of the donkey work typing the bloody thing, despite my repeated requests for a ghost writer or at least someone I can dictate to whilst lying on a chaise lounge eating grapes and drinking wine – so I suppose that the following deserve some credit:

Rosie, for putting up with me and making my life better every day; Ben for being the best boy a dad could ask for, and for having good taste in films and books and clothes; Mum, Dad, Adam

and Rebecca for being there – if you're going to
have family, at least they should be ones you like,
and thank God I'm lucky that I do; Steve Shaw
for publishing yet another of my tomes.

A tip of the hat and a double click of the bootheel
to you all.

Also by Simon Kurt Unsworth:

Novels
The Devil's Detective (Del Ray / Doubleday, 2015)
The Devil's Evidence (Del Ray / Doubleday, 2016)

Collections
Lost Places (Ash Tree Press, 2010; Black Shuck Books 2022)
Quiet Houses (Dark Continents Publishing, 2011; Black Shuck Books 2019)
Strange Gateways (PS Publishing, 2014)
Diseases of the Teeth (Black Shuck Books, 2016)
The Martledge Variations (Black Shuck Books, 2018)
Uneasy Beginnings (with Benjamin Kurt Unsworth) (Black Shuck Books, 2020)

Plays
Quiet Hauntings (Black Shuck Books, 2024)

Visit Simon Kurt Unsworth at his website:
simonkurtunsworth.wordpress.com

9 781917 173971